19.95

My Brother's Keeper

My Brother's Keeper

ERIC WRIGHT & HOWARD ENGEL

with illustrations by Greg McEvoy

McArthur & Company
Toronto

This edition published in Canada in 2002 by McArthur & Company

McArthur & Company
322 King Street West, Suite 402
Toronto, Ontario M5V 1J2

First published in September, 2001 in a limited "hors commerce" edition
by Book City in Toronto.

National Library of Canada Cataloguing in Publication

Engel, Howard, 1931-
    My brother's keeper / Howard Engel, Eric Wright.

ISBN 1-55278-327-8

I. Wright, Eric II. Title.

PS8559.N49M9 2002   C813'.54   C2002-903795-6
PR9199.3.E49M9 2002   NOV 2 2002

Text type : Cartier Book
Typesetting, printing, and binding : Coach House Printing, Toronto
Illustrator : Greg McEvoy
Editor : Kathleen Roulston
Production and design : J. Frans Donker

The publisher would like to acknowledge the financial support of the
Government of Canada through the Book Publishing Industry Development
Program (BPIDP) and the Canada Council for our publishing activities. The pub-
lisher further wishes to acknowledge the financial support of the Ontario Arts
Council for our publishing program.

10 9 8 7 6 5 4 3 2 1

ONE

"He wants me to do this one last favour, as he calls it."

Staff Inspector Charlie Salter stood sideways to the bathroom mirror and tried to suck in a belly that no longer fully retracted.

"But you've resigned, Charlie. Stand still." The week before, a dermatologist had dug a wart out of Salter's back, requiring Annie to change the dressing on the wound daily.

"Mackenzie hasn't. I thought he might go when he didn't get the chief's job. But he's gone the other way. He calls it being loyal to the force. Not getting the chief's job is just one of the lumps you take, but your first duty is to the force."

"But he never got along with the new chief, did he? That's it. You can throw away the old dressing yourself. Not down the toilet."

"He didn't when they were both deputies, no. But now Mackenzie's going to keep his personal feelings out of it, I hear. Just do his job."

"Sounds very… dedicated. Wash your hands."

"Doesn't it, though? Some bullshit there, too, though. Mackenzie doesn't have anywhere else to go. He's put out some feelers, but no one is looking for a police chief, which is what he has to have if he's going to move away from Toronto. Why am I washing my hands?"

"Because you are your own greatest single source of infection. Will your new chief trust him?"

"He might, in time. Mackenzie's making the right noises. And then, if he acts the way he talks, and the new man has a heart attack, then Mackenzie might just get to step up to the plate after all."

"Is that what he's counting on?"

"I don't think he's counting on anything, just holding his breath and doing the smart thing."

"Which is?"

"Nothing."

"And you?"

"I'm just filling in the days. I gave a month's notice, so Mackenzie's entitled to have his way with me until my time is up." He stepped on to the scales.

Annie said, "Charlie, don't get angry, but you once told me you could leave with a day's notice."

"Not in the middle of a case. I've lost a pound."

"I thought even that was possible. Not for you, though, of course. But yesterday you didn't have a case. You could have been gone by now."

"What's the rush? I'd like to wind down, get used to the idea, now that I've handed in my notice."

"We're going to the Island next month."

"This job won't interfere. If it does, I'll quit. The thing is, I've got a suspicion that this assignment comes from the chief, not from Mackenzie."

"You look a bit smug. Why you?"

Salter put his thumbs into the imaginary sleeve-holes of a non-existent waistcoat and leaned back. "It's politically sensitive," he said. "I have this reputation for tact when dealing with the movers and shakers, people we need to be careful with, politicians. That's what Mackenzie said when he gave me the job."

"There's a word for what he's calling you, you know."

"Diplomatic."

Annie let it go and moved to the bedroom to undress. "So, what is this case?" she asked over her shoulder.

"Someone's gone missing, someone they want to find before the newspapers start asking where he is."

"Disappeared?"

"Apparently. Mackenzie called me in just before I left today. The way he put it at first I was surprised it even came to us – to him, I mean. Finding missing persons has never been his job. Then he told me who it was. I still didn't really get it. Why me? There are other people and I'm in the middle of teaching Mackenzie how his word processor works. He's enjoying it, too. But when I came in this morning he told me the background. The guy who has gone missing is a big cheese in a hospital where there's already been a bit of scandal lately."

"Rose of Sharon?"

"How did you know?"

"Everybody knows. It was in the papers for a week. Now that you've retired you'll have time for the papers."

"But not the need. So the hospital, all the other hospitals, and all the associated politicos would like us to find out quickly and quietly where this guy is and bring him back. That's when I realized that the chief had told Mackenzie to put me on it. One of the hospital board members – the chairman, I guess – is connected to the woman who is hoping to become Solicitor-General, whose..."

"... Whose brother was murdered last winter."

"Right. She remembered me."

"How do you know?"

"I deduced it from the way Mackenzie beat around the bush. I don't know how happy he is to have such a celebrated detective on his staff." Salter smiled at himself in the mirror and put his thumbs back in his armpits. "I'm a mixed blessing, I would think."

"Yeah, yeah. So what are the possibilities?"

"I've been going over them. One: He's suffering from Alzheimer's and is presently on a train to Saskatoon."

"Who is he, by the way? Can I know?"

"He is chief of staff at Rose of Sharon Hospital." Salter moved back into the bedroom to get his shirt.

"So why is he on a train to Saskatoon?"

"He thinks he lives there. He did once, thirty-five years ago."

"Did anyone actually suggest Alzheimer's?"

"When a man in his sixties with no connections to Bay Street goes missing, everyone thinks Alzheimer's."

"I'll remember. What other possibilities are there? Why are you getting dressed? It's nine o'clock at night."

"He had a heart attack while he was out chasing butterflies and his body still hasn't been discovered. I don't know. I feel awake."

"Go on."

"He filled his pockets with stones and walked into Lake Ontario."

"Why?"

"Being a doctor, he couldn't avoid recognizing the symptoms of an incurable illness. Don't ask. One of his pals will tell us, if that's the answer."

"That's all the medical possibilities, then? Any others?"

"He's been mugged, or murdered."

"Is that likely? I mean, wouldn't you already know about that?"

"Someone might have planned it in a way to confuse us. Me."

"That it?"

"Well, he might just be the guy who, after an evening spent answering his wife's questions about his day, says to himself, that's enough, there has to be more to life than this, and stands up, puts on his coat, and leaves. Afterwards, his wife says she saw him walk down the street, apparently to the corner store, and then walk right past the store, turn left and disappear around the corner. No one ever sees him again. For the sake of the story, we find out that he's gone to Costa Rica where he's working as a motel clerk, living with a beautiful native girl and trying to paint." Salter put on his jacket. "Don't wait up for me."

* * *

When Salter returned an hour later, Annie asked, "Where did you go?"

"I got as far as Friday's and had a beer, but the people in the bar all looked like losers, so I came home."

"Good. Charlie, don't do things like that. Walking out without a word of explanation after thirty-eight years of marriage is very disturbing. It reminds me that I know everything about you, but I have no idea what's going on in your head."

"No one knows what anyone else thinks. You remember that play we saw in London where no one said anything; they just sat around the table farting and overhearing each other's thoughts."

"We left at intermission. Some of their thoughts were disgusting."

"That was the point, wasn't it?"

"So what's your point?"

"A man has disappeared. You asked me to suggest the possibilities. I got to the one about the guy whose life bugs him, so he leaves. That's all."

"You enjoying yourself?"

"Annie, I've been a cop slightly longer than I've been married to you. Every day after we married I came home expecting a note on the table. You know: *I can't stand this any longer. Don't try to find me.*"

"Every day?"

"For about ten years. I was very insecure. As for the job, I've had the standard worry on every case: 'How am I doing?' I've never yet concentrated purely on solving the case. Always there's the element of 'How do I look?' You know, not just, 'Am I fucking up?' but 'Is someone watching me fuck up?' That's how I define why I liked working for Orliff. As nearly as a boss could, he didn't watch me. When he left, I realized how lucky I had been. Now, lately, for a year maybe, I've been free again. I work for myself now. I don't give a shit what Mackenzie thinks of me."

"As far as I can understand you, and from what I remember of Political Science 2A, Karl Marx would have been very interested in you, and George Orwell, too. In your simple, homely way, you've been talking like a wage slave, like all wage slaves. But don't let Mackenzie hear you. You'll make him nervous."

"I don't talk like this in the office, just to you."

TWO

I had just climbed the long uninterrupted flight of stairs and unlocked the office when the telephone began ringing in that insistent way that tells you before you budge the receiver that this isn't a call to renew your subscription to the *Beacon*. There was something commanding about the ring, something strident, and if I had any sense, something to walk away from. But the familiar voice of my brother Sam on the other end of the line put me off my guard.

I swung the old office chair around so that I could listen in comfort and watch the dust motes swimming through the sunlight, as though reminding me that I should have been busy at my desk two hours ago. Sam, older than me by twenty-one months, was a doctor. He was the pride and joy of my parents, naturally, but I thought that although he made me look bad – me being a private investigator with no diploma above the desk that came from Harvard or McGill, just a licence that needed renewing – I made him look good. So we all had our parts to play in the family drama.

"Benny, how are you?"

"Between grass and hay," I said, and asked, already dreading the reply, "How are you?"

I should explain briefly that the relationship between my brother and me is one that does not include regular communication. The last time I spoke to Sam was when he phoned to tell me that Uncle Henry had died at Baycrest's Home for the Aged and that the funeral would take place the following day in Toronto. That's the Sam I expected and understood. A Sam on the phone asking "How are you?" makes me wince as I enumerate my surviving relations who are likely to require my graveside attendance. A Sam on the phone at all is enough to put a boot lock on the rest of my day.

"Benny? Are you there?"

"Must be a bad connection. Are you on one of those cell phones?"

"Jesus, Benny, things are falling apart around here. I need your help."

There it was. Another proof of the wisdom in Sam's opposition to having my parents expose my infant form on a hillside like that Greek king and Snow White's wicked stepmother. I haven't been much good to Sam; I'm a washout as a younger brother. I trailed behind him in school by two years and found that in every new class Sam's memory still shone with promise fulfilled. "Cooperman, your brother would never hand in a paper looking like that!"

"No, Mr McCaul, but I didn't have time to recopy it. I – "

"Sam never made excuses. Sam never had to make excuses. Go back to your seat."

"Yes, Mr McCaul."

"Hello? Ben, are you there?" I was still holding Sam's voice to my ear. I put aside my reflections and tried to concentrate on the here and now.

"Tell me what's going on, Sam. Tell me what you think I can do."

"I can't talk now, Benny. No such thing as a safe line, if you know what I mean. Can you come here for a couple of days?"

"To Toronto?"

"Of course, I mean Toronto. You can stay with us. It shouldn't take more than a few days to sort out." That had Sam written all over it. A "couple of days" becomes "a few days" without a blink. "A week or two" was only a breath away. The last time I spent any time in Toronto, I stayed clear of my brother. If I ran into him, I knew that the work I was doing on University Avenue would suddenly include a little gerbil-sitting and other things to remind me that I was the world's worst uncle.

"What kind of trouble is it, Sam? Hospital politics? Police business?" Sam was the Chief Surgeon at Toronto General Hospital, or so I thought. He was also a demon about fighting small traffic violations. Maybe he'd run into a judge who was unimpressed by his well-pressed suit and professional bearing. Sam spent the next five minutes explaining his recent move from Toronto General to the Rose of Sharon Hospital, which was crammed between Toronto General and the Hospital for Sick Children, all on University Avenue. As though I hadn't spent enough time on University Avenue. I hate University Avenue, with its two straight lines of traffic separated by a boulevard of flowerbeds and public monuments. Maybe if I was Albert Speer I'd like it better. I preferred the steady one-way traffic along St. Andrew Street, with The Boot Shoppe across the street and the Russell House Hotel on the corner. Grantham, in all its familiar glory.

"… So, you see, Benny, that I'm vulnerable. I'm low man on the totem pole. How soon can you get here?"

"Sam, talk sense. What do I know about hospital politics? If your chief surgeon ran off with the head nurse, maybe, just maybe, my experience might help. But give me a break, I don't have any experience in medical matters. Like that case two years ago about the kids with liver failure that the cops tried to pin on a couple of nurses."

"First of all, the head nurse has not run away with the chief surgeon. I'm the chief surgeon. She hasn't run away with anybody. It's the chief of staff. He's gone missing. Three days now. And I was the last name in his appointment book. They've called the cops, Benny. And there are a couple of people on the staff who wouldn't mind my taking the fall. I was, you might as well know, brought in over the heads of many of my new colleagues. To make matters worse, the guy who brought me to Rose of Sharon, the guy who said he'd look out for me, is the guy who's gone missing."

"Sheeee!"

"Now do you see what I mean? I'm in trouble, Benny. First time in my career. I've always watched my step and now I don't know whether to resign or what. I'm not good at this, Ben. Help a guy out?"

"How do you know yours was the last name in this guy's appointment book?"

"His name is Horner, Benny. Dr John Davidson Horner. He's as famous in his line as… as… as Fabian of Scotland Yard is in yours. He wields a lot of power around here. He's a living legend. They call him the Kingmaker."

"The appointment book?"

"What?"

"Go back to the appointment book. When did you see the appointment book? You knew you had an appointment at a certain time, right? So, you and Dr Horner agreed upon a time?"

"Irene Uhrynuk, actually."

"Huh?"

"Benny, his secretary Irene Uhrynuk made the appointment with me. She told me to come at three o'clock on Saturday afternoon."

"Isn't that unusual? Don't doctors head for Caledon Hills on weekends? I read in a magazine that they all have country houses and raise their own green vegetables beyond the suburbs near the golf courses."

"Benny, that magazine didn't talk to Davidson Horner. Horner isn't like anybody else. He works on Saturdays if he wants to. He may have done it to see if I'd come in on Shabbas."

"But you're not that observant!"

"Horner doesn't know that. Besides, he's always testing people's limits."

"Did you keep the appointment?"

"I did. He didn't. His door was open. I waited twenty minutes. Finally, I checked the book in the outer office, where Irene keeps track of things. My name was there all right, but Horner never showed up. There were no other appointments after mine. Benny, you've got to help me out."

"I still can't see how I can help out. Why don't you just wait it out? If he's gone through the keyhole with one of the nurses, it will come to light. If he ends up running a bar in North Africa, you'll hear about it in time. You just have to hold your breath."

"Nurses aren't Horner's style, Benny. Neither are orderlies. He was into power games. He liked to see himself as a big hairy spider sitting in the centre of his web, waiting for the flies and moths to come to him. Benny, I really shouldn't say more on this line. Will you come and help me out?"

"Well, I've got a few things I should be attending to."

"Please, Benny. Please!" I liked the sound of this, but I knew I couldn't stretch it out forever.

"I'll drive up in the morning, Sam. I can put a few things out to pasture for a couple of days."

"No more than a week, Ben, really. I promise you."

THREE

The next morning Salter set out to walk the three blocks between the police headquarters and Rose of Sharon Hospital, which, like most old Toronto hospitals, is situated within walking distance of University and Dundas. Toronto has plenty of other hospitals, but when old Torontonians feel a stroke coming on they tend to hail a cab and head downtown to the hospitals they grew up with.

His appointment was with one of the administrators of the hospital, a Dr Galt, whose name he had been given as the hospital's spokesperson – on missing doctors, at least. When he asked for Dr Galt, a huge woman behind a desk in the rotunda directed him to a Miss Fayad.

"Dr Galt," Salter corrected her.

"You start with Miss Fayad," the woman said in the gap between dealing with two other enquiries. In the next gap, she added, "Follow the signs to the yellow elevator and go to the second floor, Room 242."

Obediently, recognizing competence when he saw it, he followed the signs through three corridors, past a cafeteria and a gift shop, arriving at last at the yellow elevator and mounting to the second floor. Here, in Room 242, a beautiful dark-skinned woman with immaculately groomed grey hair said, "Inspector Salter? Would you wait here, please. Dr Galt will be free soon."

Salter looked at his watch. Right on time. "I'll get myself a cup of coffee down the hall while I'm waiting, shall I?"

The door behind her opened and a man in a suit appeared. "Come on in, Inspector. Some coffee? Aida, some coffee for both of us, please. Come in, come in."

He's anxious, Salter thought. Wants to please me. Why? Usually poo-bahs at this level want to show me they're not impressed, like Aida there was just trying to do.

Galt led him into the room, where another man in a suit sharper than Galt's and a tie carved into a perfect knot was getting up from his chair. Galt said, "Inspector Salter, this is Mr O'Donahue. Sir, this is Inspector Salter."

O'Donahue pressed Salter's hand between both of his. "Fred," he said. He waited a moment for a response, then, getting none, continued. "This is a one-pipe problem, I'm sure, Inspector, but we're very happy to have you with us because your chief said you had the kind of experience that would be useful." He showed all his front teeth in welcome, leaving the rest of his face blank.

Salter waited, guessing what a one-pipe problem was – the phrase had an echo – aware, too, that he was meant to see the significance of the fact that O'Donahue, whoever he was, was on terms with the chief of police, and that the chief of police, for his part, had felt it appropriate to answer this man's queries about the relative merits of his senior detectives. Salter waited. What O'Donahue and Galt didn't know yet was that no one, not even the chief, could make Salter wary of who he was talking to at this stage of his career. Salter felt great.

"So who is going to fill me in?" he asked.

"You know why you're here?" O'Donahue responded.

"Not really. A man is missing, I heard. Must be more than that, I would think."

O'Donahue switched off the powerful warm glow he had been bathing Salter in to look irritatedly at Galt.

Galt said, "I only got the call late yesterday afternoon that Inspector Salter would be here this morning."

"I talked to Chief Burnside yesterday *morning*, for Christ's sake. Well, never mind. Let's get on. He switched the warmth back on as he turned again to Salter. "What's happened here is...."

Salter put up a hand, and laboriously took out a notebook. "Can I start at the beginning, sir?" He turned to Galt. "With you, Dr Galt. You're the spokesman, right?"

Galt nodded and took a card from his desk. "Here."

Salter tucked the card away. "Now, sir, you are Mr O'Donahue.

Not a doctor."

"Fred O'Donahue." He spoke the name like a title.

Salter made a note to check up on him, make sure he wasn't a senator. "And you are?" he asked. "Your connection with the hospital, I mean, sir."

"Mr O'Donahue is acting chairman of the board of governors," Galt said.

"What else do you need to know to get going?" O'Donahue asked, irritation again overtaking his desire to charm Salter. "I'm here to make sure that we all understand how seriously the hospital takes the disappearance of Dr Horner."

"So am I. I don't usually work missing persons."

"I mean that the present situation is not of a kind that would normally involve me, but you will be aware that the hospital has lately been criticized by some politically inclined citizens. I would like whoever is officially involved in finding Dr Horner to move as quickly and quietly as possible, and to make sure that Dr Galt here is informed of anything that might give rise to bad publicity."

It was something about drugs, Salter remembered. Research. Drug companies. Doctors being paid by drug companies to do research. "I report to Deputy Chief Mackenzie," he said. "I'll tell him what you said, but he won't give me permission to report to you."

"The deputy chief? How about I talk to his boss?"

"It wouldn't make any difference. See, it's against the rules. In the meantime, let me get on. When did Dr Horner go missing?"

O'Donahue stood up. "I think I've made my point. Now I have to be elsewhere." He searched for some of his former manner. "I guess we're in good hands, eh, Galt? This guy seems to have his wits about him." He spoke as if he and Galt had been interviewing Salter for the job of security guard. It was patronizing, and, guessed Salter, meant to be.

Salter started to lumber to his feet to play the part O'Donahue had assigned him, but was halted by a gesture from O'Donahue, who then briefly clasped Salter's right hand with his own left hand, nodded to Galt, and moved quickly through the door, speaking instructions to Miss Fayad about where he could be found next.

Galt closed the door behind him. "He's a busy man," he said. "I've only seen him twice this year."

Half a dozen responses presented themselves, but Salter let them go. He said, "I'm glad I know who he is. Now, when did Dr Horner go missing?"

"Some time on the weekend. Perhaps on Sunday. We know he was in his office most of Saturday."

"That normal?

"What?"

"In his office most of Saturday. What sort of demands do you make on senior staff?"

"He probably wanted to get a report written, something like that."

"Was there any sign of a report on his desk or on his computer?"

"There was nothing on his desk, and Horner never ever used a computer. He wrote everything out longhand and his secretary typed it up. He was a shade traditional in most things."

"So who could guess what he was up to in his office on Saturday?"

"His secretary might."

"I'll talk to her. And tell me some other people to talk to."

"In what way?"

"I want to know if anyone knows where he is. I would think you will already have asked around, then stopped asking when Fred there heard about it and told you to keep it under wraps, once it was possible that something strange was going on."

"Dr Horner's sister told Mr O'Donahue that he hadn't slept in his bed since Friday night, and when she came home the Sunday *Star* was still on the porch. So Mr O'Donahue called your chief."

"I need a list, then, of the people closest to Horner, professionally and socially, and medically, I guess. I'll need to talk to them all."

"Do you mind telling me why? I know you don't have to, and I won't speculate beyond this room, but if you told me what's in your head I could provide a more focused list."

"Okay. Professionally, first. Who were his colleagues, the people he dealt with every day who knew what he was doing? Socially, who were his friends who might know whether he had bad news lately, or won a lottery. Had he been acting strangely? Medically, doctors have doctors, don't they? They aren't allowed to treat themselves, are they? Like priests can't hear their own confessions." Salter glanced up at the image of the tortured body spread on the wooden cross hanging above the door. "Who was Horner's doctor? Maybe he'd had some kind of bad news. How old was he? Sixty-three. A heart condition wouldn't be a surprise, would it? Or high blood pressure? Let alone the real baddies to do with the prostate, the colon, and what's that one, the pancreas? You guys would be hard to conceal symptoms from, wouldn't you?"

Galt had been taking rapid notes. He held up his hand. "First," he said, "Dr Horner was primarily an administrator. About twenty departments were responsible to him. I'll give you the names of two other administrators at the next level down and you can take it from there. First, there is the head of research, Dr Who."

Salter looked up to see if Galt was having a little fun with him.

Galt shook his head. "H-u-i," he said. "I think it should be pronounced Hwoy or some such, but he likes being called Dr Who."

"Was Horner a very sociable man?" Salter asked.

"Not really. I would call him a private individual. That's what you call it when a man never shares an intimacy with you, isn't it? Or with anyone else. Horner kept his secrets well."

"Or he had none."

"All right. Now you might also want to talk to the head of the medical staff, Dr Morgan. After that you'll know who else you want to see."

"Why those two?"

"I'm responding to Mr O'Donahue's concern."

"Oh, yes. That was on my list to ask you. What was the big scandal here that Fred was so uptight about?"

Galt smiled carefully at Salter's familiar way with the chairman's name. "We've had two. The first had to do with an apparent conflict of interest between a drug company and the hospital over the ownership of some research that we had conducted. Hence I'm suggesting you speak to Dr Who. The other matter concerned the qualifications of one of our residents, a man from South Africa. Both stories were in the press, by the way. I'll copy the clippings for you, save you the trouble."

"But those stories are history now, surely?"

"I'm just trying to fill you in on why Fred is uptight." Now Galt smiled properly.

"I'll take your word for them. Who else should I see? Is Horner married?"

"No. He lives with his sister. Obviously you should talk to her."

"Who was the last person to report seeing Horner?"

"One of the cleaners. Horner kept her out of his office early Saturday morning and told her not to clean his office that day."

"I'll need her name. I'll try not to look like I'm heading up a big inquiry yet, though the more time that goes by, the more likely it is that something has happened to him. I'll talk to those two doctors and then see his sister. Does she stay home? Look after him?"

"They just share a home for convenience. Call it tenants in common. You'll find her at work. She's a secretary, works for the German department at University College."

"Which is where?"

"I'm not sure. I mean, I don't have the faintest idea. Aida will know. She knows everything."

Aida did know, and Salter set off for St Joseph Street, still on foot.

FOUR

As the CN Tower loomed into view, I tried to remember what Sam told me in a late call the previous night. Dr Davidson Horner had hired Sam away from Toronto General three months ago. It was a good move, career-wise, as Sam described it, but it made a lot of people mad and some of them – some of the support staff – became deaf when he said a cheery hello in the morning. He couldn't get the time of day from anyone higher up than an orderly. Now Horner was missing and the cops had an appointment to question him about it that very afternoon.

Even discounting Sam's tendency to see himself at the centre of every drama, I warmed to his worry as he filled me in on the names and positions of the characters in this whirling hospital mystery. In our high-school production of *Hamlet*, Sam told our parents that the play was about a courtier named Osric, who was playing all the rest of the characters in the play for saps. I don't have to tell you which part he was playing. In the current drama, with him being so new to the place, at times he sounded like he was trying out to play the fool. Basically, Dr Horner had selected him, eased him into the senior management level, fought off several sorties of opposition, and then disappeared. There was a lot of vulnerability showing where Sam was concerned. And now the cops wanted to see him. Was that going to make things better?

I figured that in a town the size of Toronto, however important a hospital administrator Horner is, he's still a missing person, and nobody at the Toronto Police has time to get too excited about that after just three days. People go missing for all kinds of reasons. Usually those reasons are private, I mean they come out of his private life, not out of the way he pushed the paper across his desk. Sure, they were going to put a watching brief on the case, treat it with their most sensitive kid gloves, but in this end of the investigation, I couldn't see Sam drawing much of the heat. After all, somebody had to be last in his appointment book. Nobody could take Sam all that seriously. Everybody in Rose of Sharon hospital knows Horner better than Sam. Everybody knew that Horner had been particularly nice to Sam. Find a motive in that if you can.

* * *

The main entrance of the Rose of Sharon Hospital was closed. Scaffolding and tarpaulins were in place all over the impressive brick doorway. I found a sign inviting me and all others having business at the hospital to call around to the Emergency Wing. The sign assumed that everybody knew where that was. There was no arrow indicating whether to direct my march to the right or to the left. I followed the crowd.

An ambulance with all its lights flashing but its alarm muted crawled up the non-pedestrian side of a ramp leading to large glass windows and doors. Even in the bright light of mid-morning, the pavement under the *porte cochère* was patched with golden strips of electric light. Three other ambulances were parked at the high end of the ramp, almost hiding all of the 'no parking' signs. A mob of ambulance drivers and emergency caregivers had formed outside the entrance. I could hear raised voices as I moved up the incline.

"Not here you don't!"

"Come on! You're listed as viable."

"When you looked we were. We're full up now. Can't crowd you in, man."

"I got an elderly cardiac in the back. He doesn't have time for me to do any more hunting."

"Can't be helped. If he comes in, chances are they won't even start the paperwork until late afternoon. Man, it's a jungle in there. Half a dozen people doing the work of a small army. Believe me, you don't want to drop your cargo here. Have you tried the General?"

"Just came from there. It looks better over here."

"Shee-it, if this is better, I don't wanna see no worse!"

I moved past the ambulances and through a set of glass doors so finger-marked I thought that they had been soaped by Hallowe'en pranksters and ignored ever since. The lobby was large and crowded. The crowd diminished the proportions of the room. Right in front of me, a ten-year-old was vomiting on the floor. His mother pulled him back and tried to clean him up with a tissue. No one noticed. Bodies were huddled together in family groups, like pictures I've seen of eastern Europeans in a railway station at the peak of the holiday rush to be somewhere else. Hospital clerks worked away furiously at their stations, signing people in, collecting Health Card numbers, dealing calmly with the chaos. A man with a pair of scissors stuck in his thigh, the scissors attached to his ripped jeans with adhesive tape, as though it was likely to go anyplace by itself, was seated in a wheel-chair with a policeman standing behind it. A woman with two swollen forearms was staring at the ceiling, her face stained with tears; a small child was tugging at her coat. A man in a leather motor-cycle outfit was sitting between two policemen with his face buried in his hands. Bundles of humanity everywhere and not a doctor in sight. Side by side in plastic chairs, a man held a bloodstained hand-kerchief up to his right eye. The blood had spattered his white shirt, while his neighbour held a clearly broken right arm in place with the left, while whimpering softly. A security guard was holding the wrist of a man wearing a pajama top and holding a small baby in his free arm. He was shouting in a language neither I nor the guard under-stood. I tried to push my way through the mass, getting a glimpse of a woman on a gurney, her clothes in disorder around her. She was attached to an IV stand and to a monitor that was sending pointed lines up and down the screen. Nobody had thought to pull a curtain across the opening to the cubicle. Groans came from other blue-masked cubicles.

"I've got a *grand mal* seizure in number six and cardiac arrest in eight! Where is the resident?"

Before that cry for help was answered, I found the main corridor and made my escape from the war zone. The long and cool terraz-zoed corridor looked more like my idea of a hospital, except for the stretchers and gurneys parked along the walls on both sides. I made

my way to the Information Desk, where a clerk consulted a register to find Sam's name. "He'll be on the fourth floor, Centre Block," she said. "Take the elevators over there. Have a good day." She pointed to the block of elevators, and saw that the button had already been pushed; it shone with a pale yellow light and remained shining for another five minutes without delivering on its unspoken promise. I looked at the indicator, one of the old-fashioned kind with a brass arrow, which told me that the elevator was stuck on the seventh floor, where it stayed for a full two minutes. Other cars further up were progressing incrementally: 9, 10, 11, 12, 14. I began thinking of taking the stairs and looked around for them. None in sight. I examined the faces of the oil-painted hospital benefactors along the panelled walls of the main entrance lobby. Through the still-revolving doors I could see the back of the scaffolding I'd earlier seen from the reverse angle.

At last the wait in front of the elevator was over, or at least it seemed to be over. The car disgorged a mighty hoard, all headed in different directions: busy people with things to do. The car itself, still partly populated, continued downward to service several layers of basements. When the crowd I was standing in finally moved into the up elevator, it swept me along with it. I was hard pressed to get my floor button pushed and was unprepared when the door opened behind me.

Surrounding the elevators, the powers that be in the hospital had tried to add decorations to an ordinary hospital corridor to give it class: wood panelling with portraits and citations of merit beside flags and a framed picture of Queen Elizabeth, who had cut a ribbon for a new wing a few years ago. Here and there a few easy chairs were set out to create a cosy nook. For everybody else, there were waiting rooms.

I followed instructions and soon found myself outside Sam's office, or what I thought was Sam's office. It contained an empty desk and almost enough room to get around it to sit in the chair. The other chair had to be moved to close the door. A voice behind me boomed, "Yes?" I turned to see a trim, well-dressed black woman manœuvre around me to find her usual place behind the grey metal desk. I explained who I was and she introduced herself as Monica Levine. She looked nicer than most of the Levines I know in Grantham, but I recognized that it was an unexpected surname. She was wearing a tan suit over a deep blue blouse. Her hair was tightly secured at the back of her well-shaped head. "He's in a meeting right now, but I'll tell him you're here." He'd told me that he was meeting the police. But that was the day before. This had to be another meeting.

"Is there somewhere I can wait?"

"Sure," she said dubiously. "But I think he's going to be tied up for an hour at least. These things are never short." She said this to me like I was a fellow-sufferer of hospital administration-itis. Then she brightened. "Why don't you go right across and wait in his office?"

"If that's not breaking a rule or something?"

"We got so many rules nowadays nobody notices when any get broken. It's more comfortable in there and there's less chance of you getting interrupted."

"It's as bad as that, is it?"

"Don't get me talking about that. The door's almost across the hall. His name's on it."

I thanked Monica by name, not knowing what her title might be or whether Miss, Ms or Mrs was appropriate. She got up and moved out from behind her desk as I made it out into the corridor ahead of her. She skirted around two parked gurneys, then pointed. "That's the door there," she said. As I was reaching for the door knob, I could see that Monica had moved on to confer with an orderly wheeling a populated gurney from the middle of the corridor to look for a parking space along the wall.

"Monica," I called. As I was about to shut Sam's door, I felt a moment of panic. I called Monica's name, only half-realizing that she might follow up.

"Was that you calling, Mr Cooperman, or my overcrowded conscience?" I backed into the room, and she followed me.

"I was wondering whether you could give me a short course in this hospital's administration. Who's the boss, for instance? Who does Sam answer to? Who should I avoid if I want to keep Sam's name out of the papers? Stuff like that."

"Poor lamb, he didn't tell you much, I guess?"

"Less than you guess."

"Okay, then, let's see. The name of the missing man is Horner. John Davidson Horner. He practically built this hospital. He's the CEO, but, between us, he's not been carrying the full load. He's on the board of directors, but the chairman of the board is Fred O'Donahue. The chief public relations officer, I forget his real title, is Dr Galt, Francis Galt. He's a bit of a rabbit, runs scared if there's a whisper of scandal in the corridors. His record of keeping the press in their places is only so-so. We've had two recent scandals, which have dragged on for the last six months. The papers are really tired of them, so they only print new, sensational stuff. I'll talk to Irene Uhrynuk, Horner's secretary. She can give you all the scoop on Horner. You'll want to talk to her. I'll set it up."

"Great!"

"You may want to talk to Dr Paul Hui and Dr Ivor Morgan."

"Who are they? People who knew Horner, I guess. I don't have to know whether they slice or stitch, do I?" Monica smiled, told me she'd write it down for me, and waved me goodbye. I figured that Monica could be a wellspring of gossip about the hospital, but that she was rationing herself to the most helpful bits right now. I waved uncertainly as she faced me while she was closing the door.

Sam's office was not the *sanctum sanctorum* of the wise old doctor in the movies. There were no book-lined walls, or even bell jars with nasty-looking specimens inside. I've seen policemen with better decorated offices. It was roomy enough, but the effect was one of haste and some confusion. Cardboard boxes of books and files lay everywhere. Nails that had once supported diplomas or pictures stood empty, drawing attention to the dusty wall space around them.

I waited five minutes. I tried to think of the fifty-five minutes more I had to put in. I was too restless. I got up, looked around again. In a cupboard I found a parka with fur trim, a red plaid hunting jacket, and, under everything, a white medical coat, which gave me an idea. I put the coat on, slipped a face mask around my neck casually, buttoned up, and grabbed a clipboard and pencil. In a mirror, I thought

I looked the part. If questioned, I hadn't an idea what I would say. Maybe that I was chilly?

Anyway, in that hour, I covered the hospital from the second basement, checking out the tunnels leading to the other hospitals on University Avenue. On the sixteenth floor I found a well-appointed lounge being used by families or friends of patients having serious surgery. Two people asked if there was any news. I shook my head and hurried on. Near the door, a surgeon, fresh from an operating room in green summer-weight working clothes, was telling an elderly couple: "I'm ninety-five percent sure we got it all." The grey-haired man held the woman's arm tightly.

"Thank God," she said, as I continued down the corridor.

Two floors down I found a staff cafeteria. It was no Diana Sweets, but it was smoke-free and bustling. I got them to make me a fresh chopped egg sandwich on white, rejecting the sandwich on brown with curly edges. I helped myself to a container of milk from the glass-fronted cooler. Then I carried my tray, scouting for a clear space. I shifted a tray or two, made room, sat down, and started making notes. When I'd settled in, I thought that a cup of coffee would go down well after the sandwich and milk. Besides, by that time it would be cool enough to drink. Like a lot of people, I've gotten used to drinking coffee lukewarm or cold. It's occupational. I don't even think about it much. I decided to eke out the time with my clipboard, making notes. Milk is fine for meals, but coffee is better to think on. I put Sam's name at the top of the page, smiled smugly at myself, and then crossed it out. This was Horner's case, not Sam's. Sam comes into it through a side door. Horner's last appointment need not be significant. If he hadn't disappeared, no one would think anything of it. "Disappeared," I muttered aloud, then continued more introspectively: What does that mean? Was he kidnapped? Marched at gunpoint to a waiting car and driven off to a shack somewhere? Too much like a Saturday matinée at the Granada Theatre. Well, held in a house in the suburbs, then? Still too melodramatic. More likely he has, as I told Sam, "gone through the keyhole with a pretty face. It happens to older men. Remember the story of the Grantham radio announcer saying that he was too much in love with life to waste it in Grantham

In a mirror, I thought I looked the part.

when Paris was out there. Paris and London and Rome! He's now doing weather reports in Woodstock. It takes more than a few draughts of beer to sustain a real breakaway. Like the guy in the Hammett book, *The Maltese Falcon*. Forget his name, but he ran away from his life after nearly being killed by a falling grand piano or safe or something. Changed his life, left his wife, kids, job, house, car, and bolted. When Sam Spade caught up to him a couple of years later, he'd created his former life all over again, like God did for Job. Seems after the first big shock that woke him up to the reality of his ordinary life, he got used to the fact that grand pianos or safes don't fall out of the sky every day. So he slipped back into his rut, a different rut, as comfortable as the first one.

Back to Horner. Concentrate on him. You've got to ask Sam to tell you all he knows about him. People don't overthrow habits of a lifetime without a good reason. Remember Harry Williman? Insurance salesman, with his office over Herzog's Men's Wear? He told me a dozen times that he was going to ditch his wife and "light out to the territory," whatever that meant. He did take off, he told me, but when he crawled back, from Buffalo, I think it was, nobody knew that he'd been away.

"Dr Cooperman, I presume?"

I heard the words behind me. They stabbed me in the back. I turned slowly around.

FIVE

"So far," Salter said, "Dr Horner's only missing. But for a man in his position to be missing, even for a day, means that something is probably wrong, wouldn't you say? He was your boss. You dealt with him on a daily basis, right?" Salter was talking to Dr Morgan, the head of the medical staff.

"We spoke daily by phone at least."

"Then tell me what to suspect."

"I haven't the faintest idea. Suspecting is your speciality, isn't it? Mine is endocrinology, or it used to be." Morgan was a little man with bad skin, a fussy manner, and a loud bass voice. The combination was odd, giving the impression of a villain in an animated cartoon.

Salter said, "You worked with him, you spoke with him daily for a year, at least? Five years? Okay. And you are a doctor, trained to notice all those little changes in appearance and behaviour that indicate that a patient is diseased, poisoned, or losing his marbles. That right?"

"I suppose so."

"Well, then, if I promise not to quote you, would you tell me if you noticed anything odd about your boss in the last few weeks, especially the last few days."

"Something that might bear on his disappearance, you mean?"

"That's what we're here for."

"Then, no."

"And he never confided anything to you about his health?"

"He was a very private man."

"So I've been hearing. Who was his doctor? Someone told me this morning that doctors have doctors just like the rest of us."

"It's hard to look down your own throat."

Or get your own finger up, thought Salter, who had just suffered this annual indignity. "Do you know who he was?"

"He and I have the same man, Blostein."

Salter grinned. "Small world."

"He's yours, too? "Morgan smiled.

"Toronto's just a village, didn't you know? What are the ethics here, doctor? Would it be possible for you to speak to Blostein personally, nothing to do with me, but so as to save me a lot of trouble?"

Now Morgan revealed his back molars in his pleasure at being invited into Salter's world. "It is totally unethical, but why don't you go for a walk. Come back in five minutes."

Salter walked along the corridor to find a washroom, then returned to find Morgan prepared for him.

"Don't waste your time with Blostein," he said. "Or go ahead, waste your time." He stopped and flashed the wolfish grin to show he knew he had delivered a little paradox, and Salter left.

* * *

Dr Hui was a fundraiser. In this first exchange he told Salter that he had hardly any contact with Horner. "I go out collecting money," he said, pointing to a fat, battered briefcase lying on his desk, presumably full of money. "They call me The Bagman. There's a whole team of us, of course, working for the board ultimately, but I'm the head honcho. I haven't seen much of Horner lately – you think he's dead? – and to tell you the truth, not much in the past, either. I don't hang around the labs much, or the wards, but I can bring in the guy who can help, if anyone can. Name of Bardell. Anyone mention him? Dr Bardell? He's in my division, working on a special project, really on his own, creating a drug-testing program. By 'special' I don't mean extraordinary, just that it isn't part of our normal work. Bardell suggested it himself and collected the funds to work on it. The reason he might help, though, is that he is sort of a protégé of Horner's. Horner brought him to me because Bardell wanted to do this work he had found the money for by himself, and at the same time move to Toronto from Bracebridge, where he couldn't find the facilities he wanted. Horner knew Bardell's family from way back and took an interest in him. If anyone knows Horner it will be Bardell. Shall I set it up? An hour? Hold on." Morgan made a phone call, talked to Dr Bardell, and it was done. "Eleven-thirty, in his lab. Okay?" Morgan gave the directions.

* * *

"He took an interest in me when I was in medical school here. He was in charge of teaching at the hospital then. He learned somehow that I was thinking of dropping out for lack of money and he quietly, almost anonymously, supplied the money I needed to carry on. He said the money came from a discretionary fund that some private benefactor had set up for him, but I've often thought since that it was probably his own money. Whatever it was, I was and am deeply grateful and pretty sick about what might have happened to him. Dr Bardell took off his glasses and polished them, the classical gesture of a man moved. He pushed them back on his nose. "What can I do to help?" he asked.

"What do you know of his private life?"

"In what sense? His – er – intimate life?"

"I want to know what was troubling him, if anything. Money, for instance."

"There is no secret life, I'm sure. With Dr Horner what you see is what you get. I'm sure he has no money problems, and others will tell you if he has medical problems, which I doubt. The only possibility I can think of is that someone, something, surfaced from the distant past which none of us knows anything about. If so, it must have been a long while ago because his colleagues here – and his sister, of course – will vouch that he leads a blameless life and has done so for thirty years or more, since they've known him. I think possibly, in writing that book of his – you know about the book? – that he might have gone too far and someone called him on it. You know, medicine is unlike anything else. There are circumstances that create situations, mistakes, that can wreck a career, quite unfairly, and cover-ups happen."

"And sometimes they can go on for a long time. After a dozen people are dead you call us in."

"It can happen that we are so reluctant to believe it that no one blows the whistle until much too late. I've been thinking about this book of his; writing it at all is not very wise, even though there's not much chance of its getting published. Perhaps he was silly enough to check the details of an old incident in such a way that the person or persons involved in the incident realized that what he or they believed was ancient history is being dug up and coming back to ruin them."

"So he, or they, kill him?"

"He or they might move to protect themselves from having an incident from the past come out, without going that far."

"Threaten him, you mean?"

"Yes. That's what I mean. Sort of checkmate him. Say to him, if you publish that book, I'll tell a story I know. About an incident in Horner's student days, accounting for why he's a bachelor. The incident need not be true, as long as it's believable and hard to disprove easily. I know Dr Horner well. He's a man of extraordinary probity, eccentrically upright, you might say. Even though he could see that he would be badly damaged he would not succumb to threats. He would expose the threatener, or try to, and it would be too late to carry out the threat or withdraw it. Horner would move to have the man kicked out."

"So Dr X, whoever he is, kills him?"

"Or Dr Horner kills himself, knowing that the rumour will finish him. I thought of that, too."

"Christ. Did you dream this up all by yourself, out of thin air?"

"Out of my knowledge of Dr Horner's character."

SIX

"Dr Cooperman, I presume!" the voice had said. I turned around slowly, wondering what I was going to say. If it was someone who thought I was Sam, that was one thing. I could say that he was mistaken. If he had fathomed my impersonation of eight years of medical school, I was sunk. When my eyes focused on a similarly white-coated figure, holding my breath all the while, I was able to let it out again. It was Sam.

"Sam! Don't do that! You want me to have cardiac arrest right here and now?"

"Name a better place for it?" He was grinning like an older brother, benign, hateful.

"Forget about public relations for five minutes, I read the papers; I saw your Emergency Room. Don't try to kid me out of a genuine heart attack. When I have a coronary, I'll do it at home, where I'll have some chance of surviving it."

"We're not as black as we are painted, Benny. Why, I discharged a patient this morning. I sent him home. He was cured." Sam put his hands in the front pockets of his white coat, instinctively ferreting for the absent cigarettes. A grin began to spread across his face. "Thanks for coming." He took my hand and set down a mug of coffee across from my chilling one. "You look good in that coat," he said. You could have fooled anyone but me. And with me, your secret is secure. I won't call the cops."

"Hey! On whose behalf do you think I put on this disguise?"

Sam took a sip from his cup.

"Sam, tell me about Horner. I need to know what you know about him."

"Ah, yes. Where to begin?"

"When did you first hear of him?"

38

"That's easy. In medical school. Horner was famous. Not only did he have this huge reputation in medicine, but he was a mover and shaker. He could get people and institutions to part with big bucks to further his plans for this hospital. He was a super-salesman for the Rose of Sharon. He got the building, the underpinnings that sustain it. That's one side of him. The part we heard about when we were interning was that he was a kingmaker. Kingmaker became his nickname. He watched us. He paid attention during general rounds and found places for those he wanted to help. He sent Joe Calnan to Johns Hopkins; Mike Prescott – you remember Mike from Granthan? – he sent Mike to McGill with his blessing. And a blessing from John Davidson Horner carried a lot of weight. I mean, nobody wanted to default on a recommendation from the Kingmaker. We all did very well. And it's a funny thing about Horner, he recommended the best, as I say, but he's a man of his time. He is full of racial and religious prejudices. Top to toe. He comes out with the most politically incorrect statements all the time. Hell, if he wasn't Horner, they'd have got rid of him long ago, just because he's become a public embarrassment to people like Fred O'Donahue and the rest of the hospital board. But – and this is what I was going to say – he picks his favourites with an eye that sees no colours or religions. It's amazing. In a meeting he'll go on about Chinese drivers and Jewish gouging, naked Hottentots with bones in their noses, and Italian lawlessness as though he were back in the 1930s, when you could hear that kind of talk all over the country."

"Curious character."

"When I say that his decisions were free from prejudice, I don't mean he was a pussycat. He was a tough man in a meeting. He hung onto his opinions with a stubbornness you wouldn't believe. He defended the Rose of Sharon against the Catholic Church itself! And he's United Church, for God's sake!"

"Is he usually at loggerheads with the Church?"

"Ah, let's say they've come to an accommodation. They put O'Donahue on the board to make sure that some medical procedures, if they are performed, don't get into the papers."

"Well, I don't see the Vatican taking a hand in Horner's disappearance. Still, nobody expects the Spanish Inquisition." I caught my breath and tried to think of more questions. Over the years I've discovered that the number of answers you get often depends on the number and quality of the questions you ask. "I thought that chairman of the board was almost an honorary position. O'Donahue seems very hands on. Is there a reason?"

"Sure. Horner's not just anybody at Rose of Sharon. But he's slightly in decline. As CEO, he can't quite hack it anymore. O'Donahue's been trying to release him from the routine administrative chores, so that he can still function in the areas left for him."

"Horner happy with that?"

"As far as I know. He gets along with the board. There are only the usual boardroom problems, nothing unusual."

"Tell me about his private life."

"I don't know much about that. He doesn't talk about it. I think he has some club or clubs he belongs to. I'm not your best source on that."

"Is there a Mrs Horner?"

"He's a bachelor, or a widower; don't know which. Lives with a relative."

"Who should I talk to about that?"

"His secretary, I guess. Irene Uhrynuk. She's fiercely loyal to Horner, but she might open up to you under the circumstances."

"Who else should I talk to?"

"You should try Ivor Morgan or Clive Bardell. They've been here at least ten years, probably more, and Bardell is close to Horner. One of his boys."

"Boys?" I asked, lifting an eyebrow.

"You're not going to get off that easy, Benny. Davidson Horner was straight as a poker. Some of his choicest politically incorrect comments were reserved for members of the gay community. No, you're going to have to work harder than that. And Bardell's straight, too. Bit of a lady's man. But he was very helpful to me when I landed here without knowing anybody. Morgan's stiff and formal, but he's honest."

"You haven't had an easy time of it. Has it been three months?"

Sam nodded ruefully.

"Tell me about that."

"Horner brought me in over the heads of everybody. I thought that he had smoothed the way, but I was a very controversial appointment. O'Donahue waved the old quota flag, saying 'But we already have Joe Cohen, and Sidney Levenson.' That sort of thing."

"In this day and age? I don't believe it."

"Oh, it doesn't go down on paper that way. I'm talking about the rough and tumble of the discussion. They don't leave primitive fingerprints where they're sure to be discovered, Benny. In the end, the rest of the board prevailed, but I didn't see many friendly faces when I arrived."

"Because you're Jewish?"

"That was only a small part of it. Because I was from outside, because I was parachuted here in one of Horner's more high-handed ploys. When I got here, I couldn't get anyone to tell me where the surgeon's lounge was. And when I made a boo-boo, the whole hospital knew about it. Once it got into the papers. A leak from a very well-informed but anonymous source."

"Left scissors inside a patient again, did you?"

"What do you mean again? No, it wasn't anything surgical, thank God; it was a few procedural or administrative bad calls. Then, when what was off the record appeared in the paper, my ass was under the guillotine."

"Ouch! Was that the worst of it?"

"There were a few smaller things, petty, really. I saved a nurse from losing her job when she mixed up some drugs."

"Was that a good idea? Was it incompetence?"

"Benny, now don't you start! It was my call and I'll stand behind it. What these incidents add up to, Benny, is that I am the least popular member of the senior staff. There's nobody here who I can trust absolutely. Not only am I low man on the greasy pole, I'm the new boy without a map."

"Tell me about the small, petty things, Sam. It'll be good for you."

"I drew stationery from the coffin – that's what they call the big cabinet full of office supplies – without signing for it. Nobody told me! I made the sort of phone calls that I made every day at the General, only to discover that at Rose of Sharon 'we do things differently.'"

"You can't draw a new pencil without showing the stub of the previous one?"

"That sort of thing. My secretary – you met Monica? Monica Levine? Well, she steered me past most of the obstacles. She's a smart woman and she knows this place."

"First, have you met with the cops yet? They can be a pain in the neck if you rub them the wrong way."

"Yeah. They sent this old guy, Salter. Inspector. He must be ready for retirement. They're getting their pound of flesh before putting him out to grass. To mix a metaphor."

"What? Never mind, what did he want to know from you?"

"The same things you're asking. Says he's getting the runaround by O'Donahue and the board. Bardell was some help. He's off his turf here, but he's smart and, at the moment, I'm the off-side player."

"What does he think you did with him? Threw him away with amputated legs and gall bladders?"

"That occurred to him. But, for now, he's just collecting information. Benny, remember, real cops aren't like the cops on television: they ask questions, they don't answer them. They aren't big on explaining why. And Salter only told me what I've just repeated to get on my good side. I don't expect him to come to me with news of all the latest developments."

"Very sound technique. Very Aylmer Police school of case management. I'm impressed."

"Just try to stay out of his way. And by the way, Sue is expecting you for dinner tonight. The girls haven't seen their Uncle Benny for too long. You won't recognize them."

Katey and Lynn were my only nieces. I try to be a good uncle, but I fail every time. Families, even my own, are abstractions once they're out of sight. I tried to think of Katey's gerbil, Cactus Jack. (I'd babysat Cactus Jack – the first of many, I suspect – a couple of years ago.) That helped bring both the girls into focus. It was a focus on the past, as it turned out. Sam was right: both of them had grown several inches since the last time I played uncle. I saw that when I turned up for dinner that night. I'll come to that later. Meanwhile, my first day on the job was a long way from being over.

SEVEN

"He didn't have to explain if he wanted to use the office on Saturdays."

Salter was having lunch with Horner's sister, a half-pint of Guinness and a hamburger for her, a bottle of Upper Canada lager and a bowl of chili for him, in the Lexington, an imitation English pub two blocks from her office, the place and occasion suggested by her. "I can't talk to you here," she had said, when he called her office. "There are no withdrawing rooms in this college. We could go to the Faculty Club or to Massey College, but both of them are stronger on collegiality than food at lunchtime, so buy me a beer and a sandwich at the Lexington – you know it? There are lots of odd corners where we can find a discreet spot, and if you aren't sure where it is, it's unlikely you'll see anyone you know, if that matters. Make it sharp at twelve, or even five to, so we can choose a spot with our backs to the wall."

He made sure to be first so he could get a look at her while she was looking around the room for him. She was, he guessed, about fifty, a stocky woman with an alert air who continually glanced around her even when she was seated, as if she wanted to keep tabs on the whole room. She spoke, glanced about, spoke again, then resurveyed the room. Even when she was concentrating hard she found the need to look away suddenly, as if she had heard a familiar voice a few feet to one side of Salter. He had the impression that the mannerism had been acquired a very long time ago, perhaps as a student keeping her wits about her in a seminar. Her hair had been fair once, but was now mostly grey, chopped off level with her ear-lobes. Her top teeth were braced with a wire, which Salter found endearing. She was slightly wrinkled about the eyes, but her skin at fifty (?) was that of the woman in the face-cream advertisements who was still prepared to enter a guess-which-one competition with her married daughter.

Salter said, "Did he have regular habits?"

"Was he regular in his habits? Yes. Militarily so, you might say."

"So why did he go to work this Saturday? Not usual, you say, was it?"

"I have no idea at all. It's obviously the most important clue. Find the answer and you will have the end of Ariadne's thread to lead you through the maze."

"And back."

"That's the point of Ariadne's thread."

Hearing it twice, Salter felt sure of an approximate spelling and he wrote it down to ask Annie about later. He took a sip of his beer. "Tell me about your brother's personal life."

"I'll start with a synoptic sketch, shall I? You zero in on anything that looks promising."

"That would be fine."

"First, Davidson is a bachelor."

"I see."

"Do you? What do you see?"

"Nothing. I meant just 'Uh-huh.' What else?"

"Good, because the reason he is a bachelor is not the one that leaps to mind these days. As far as I know – I grew up with him and I've lived with him for these last twenty years – he is a bachelor because he is unencumbered by the physical and emotional needs of the rest of us. He's a freak. Now, if he appears tomorrow with a plausible explanation for his disappearance I ask you to forget this conversation in which I am only trying to save you useless speculation. But I don't think he will."

"Reappear tomorrow?"

"There is no possible reason that isn't sinister why he has disappeared."

Salter affected to ignore this. "What were his routines?"

"His life? He worked at the hospital, and he had three leisure pursuits. He belonged to a dining club, which met every two weeks on a Friday night. They dined in a Greek restaurant out on the Danforth, near the Chester subway station. They called themselves 'The Old

Shavers,' and they went in for a lot of parliamentary tomfoolery. They debated motions and interrupted each other with cries of 'Order.' You know – schoolboy stuff. Lots of rules."

"Do you know who else was in the group? How many?"

"About twenty. Mostly widowers and bachelors, plus one or two husbands who preferred this sort of thing to staying home with their wives. Davidson didn't take it seriously. None of them did – of course, they weren't intended to – but I mean it wasn't as important to him as it was to some of them. It was sort of like an Old Boys club. I agree with those who think men grow up more slowly than women."

"Was he close to anyone in the group, closer than to the others?"

"Not really. It was just a bit of relaxation after a hard week's work. He belonged to a much more serious dining club that met on the first Wednesday of each month to hear a paper given by one of the members. This one Davidson found very stimulating. They were all professionals of various sorts – I mean they belonged to professions, not that they were highly skilled – and the papers they gave grew out of their area of knowledge, but they were traditionally unconventional or more speculative than they might be in public. There are academics, medical people – men, that is; there are no women in that group – writers, all sorts. For example, Davidson heard his first attack on Freud's integrity in this group. The man giving the paper was quite sure of his grounds, but his argument wasn't in publishable form as yet."

"Could you give me some of their names?"

"Certainly. Later. Remind me. Then there is a third group. Once a month Davidson joins a literary lunch table – mostly editors and publishers who come together to gossip about literary matters. They have a rule – their only rule – that nothing said in the room should be repeated outside. Davidson loved that one. He's the only non-literary person in the group. He says he feels at home there. I think he means that he is more interested in literature than he is in medicine. He has a reputation as a brilliant medical man, but he isn't, just a colossal over-achiever, which is why he went into administration as soon as he could. You get the same thing in the academic world."

"How did he become a member of this group?"

"An editor in the group had heard that he was writing a book, a sort of history of the hospital, and she approached him a few years ago, or he approached her, I don't know, but at any rate she was on the hospital's board at the time, you know, the 'citizen-at-large' seat – Vera Denbigh is her name – a Czech woman, got out during one of the scuffles after the war, came here and married a local financier, chap rich as a Mafia godfather. I've met him at a drinks party and asked him if his name indicated a Welsh background, but he told me his family came from a North Yorkshire village, so there you are. After they married, she set up as a publisher. I know all this because she was once a student at University College, admitted without the usual qualifications, refugee and all that, into the honours English program. Four years later she graduated at the top of the class, speaking perfect English with a slight mid-European accent. Actually, the name sounds more Roumanian to me. In any case, it complements her rather striking looks. But I'm straying from your question. How did Davidson become a member? You'll have to ask Vera Denbigh. She invited him to be her guest at a meeting of the Boswell Club, the lunch club. You see the point? Literary gossip – he was enchanted with it. He felt like a guest at a salon, as he told me, and before she knew it he was suggesting to Vera that she should put him up for membership."

"What are the plans for publishing the hospital story now?"

"You'll have to ask Vera about that."

"Okay, tell me about the last weekend."

"I went away. You knew that. A weekend in Alqonquin Park, at a lodge with a friend. The weather was lovely and we had just the weekend we hoped for. When I came home on Sunday I saw that Arthur wasn't there and had not slept there on Saturday night, so on Monday I called the hospital to find he hadn't arrived for work. They did a check for me. None of the local hospitals had admitted Davidson or any stranger who looked like him over the weekend. So now we had a mystery and a possible tragedy. That's when the hospital got in touch with O'Donahue and he called your chief."

"When did you leave for the weekend?"

"About ten on Saturday. We wanted to let the morning traffic to cottage country subside a bit, not spend all weekend on Highway 11. Besides, my friend had things to do which kept us back until after breakfast."

"Your brother was still at home then?"

"Oh, yes. I reminded him about Samson, the cat, who needed to be let out briefly, and then back in. Samson doesn't like it outside. And I changed our beds and put the sheets into the washing machine, reminding Davidson to put them in the dryer at some point during the day. That's how I know he never slept in the bed on the weekend. And Samson was hungry when we got back on Sunday night, so he hadn't been fed either."

Salter said, "Another Guinness?"

"Certainly. It might settle me a bit. Davidson's disappearance looks bad, doesn't?"

"Too soon to speculate."

"No, it isn't. That's a cliché. It's too soon to *know*, but I've been speculating, gloomily, ever since I came home. Something's happened to him."

"Will you be all right at home, alone?"

"I've arranged for a friend to stay over for a few days."

"The friend you were with in Algonquin Park – have you spoken to her?"

"It's no business of yours, Mr Salter, but my Algonquin Park friend is male. He's my fiancé. He's a librarian at the Robarts. We're waiting to move his mother into a nursing home so we can sell their house and get married."

"Are you your brother's housekeeper?"

She laughed. "Yes, I am. Without me he would live on frozen food. But not for much longer. I want to be married and that's that."

As often before in an investigation, Salter had stumbled into an area far more interesting than what he was supposed to be investigating. Did the married pair plan to live with Horner after they married? Or would they get a new house with a granny flat for him?

She said, "I might as well tell you the story. My fiancé looks after his aged mother because there's no one else. She has her wits about her, very much so, but she's in her late eighties and getting frail. He won't consider moving her into a nursing home until she's an invalid. So there it is."

"She doesn't know about you?"

"We are not simpatico. That's her word, and she actually uses it. 'We are not simpatico,' she says, pronouncing it correctly. Yes, she knows about me, but she ignores the situation. Then there's Davidson."

"He knows about your fiancé, surely."

"Of course. And he's made it clear that he thinks I should get married and leave him alone. His intentions are kind, but he won't allow my fiancé to stay over, and I can't stay the night at my fiancé's house. We are like married adulterers, a situation I detest. But I don't think a weekend in Algonquin Park in the fall is the same as a night in a motel, is it?"

The question wasn't rhetorical, but more of a plea for his agreement. Salter allowed a moment of silence to show he had heard it properly. "Does the rest of the world know about you and your fiancé?" he asked.

"We bump into people in restaurants. You're bound to in Toronto. Yes, the world has begun to be aware, and they see me, I expect, as a slightly comic figure, in love at my age, but unable to get the freedom to marry. Mrs Gaskell could have done something with it. Now let me remind you, Inspector, I am telling you this to save you the trouble of learning it in bits and pieces. You might as well go armed with knowledge when you are grilling people. It will help you to judge their responses. Remember that James and I never say a word to anybody about our situation."

"Tell me what to do," Salter said suddenly.

"Tell you your job, you mean?"

"If you like. I could ask questions all afternoon and still not hit upon the real ones. You can ask better ones than me. You've lived with Davidson most of your life. What are his routines? For example, when his day at the hospital is finished, does he drive home?"

"He doesn't drive, didn't I say that?"

"No. So he catches a bus? The Avenue Road one?"

"No. He walks through to Yonge Street along College and takes

48

the subway north to Summerhill, then walks north to our street. Sometimes he calls in to the liquor store, or to one of those stores nearby for something I need. I do most of the shopping on weekends, but he might pick up some bread or vegetables if I call him."

"And that's his routine, every day."

"That's what routine means, surely. Very occasionally, if I haven't already gone with my fiancé, we would go to a movie together. Then we would go to a restaurant first – he likes Hannah's Kitchen opposite the Cineplex at Eglinton. That happens perhaps once a month. Then, as I said, he meets regularly with his dining club, and I won't expect him until ten-thirty or eleven. On Friday nights I cook dinner for James, my fiancé, a little domestic 'at home' evening."

"So what would you guess happened on Saturday night?"

"I think he was kidnapped. Abducted."

"You don't think he became ill suddenly?"

"You haven't come across him, have you? It isn't as if he had to walk through the forest. It's about three blocks along College Street, which is very brightly lit, and part of the way takes you past the police headquarters, and then it's two blocks from Summerhill, also pretty brightly lit and busy, to our house."

"You haven't noticed any signs of strain lately?"

"Unusual behaviour? No. He flew out to Winnipeg last Wednesday. He said he wanted to talk to an acquaintance – by Davidson's reclusive standards, a close friend – a doctor we had met on a cruise around the Greek Islands. Did I tell you he and I generally take holidays together? My fiancé's mother won't let anyone else look after her – did I tell you that, too? Two years ago Davidson struck up a bit of a friendship with this other doctor on our cruise, a urologist from Winnipeg.

That was the only break in Davidson's routine for the last six months, as far as I can remember. It wasn't that extraordinary. He did occasionally go off on his own, to conferences and such, or to visit a hospital that had instituted a new way of admitting patients that he was curious about."

"I have to ask my next question..."

"No, you don't. I know we are all capable of being surprised by our nearest and dearest, but I would swear that Davidson had no secret life, sexual or in any other way furtive, that might have drawn him away from well-lit streets."

"Then where is he?"

"In the hospital somewhere, dead. Suffered a heart attack, fell down somewhere out of sight. It's the only possibility."

EIGHT

In passing Sam's office door, I detoured inside long enough to doff my disguise, which Sam acknowledged was at least as good as my Old Gobbo costume. Now, turned out like a private investigator, wearing a jacket and tie, I felt conspicuous. In hospitals, the normal social order of dress is reversed: the surgeon in his sweaty greens outranks the three-piece suit, and a shirt and tie cuts you no slack at all. Sam said he would think of something to give me an edge. Keeping the clipboard might do it.

We stopped outside the door to Monica Levine's tiny office. She was crowded into the corner so she wouldn't be hit by the opening of the door. If you didn't watch yourself, you could collect a few bruises in a day.

"Hi, there!" she said, pivoting around from her computer monitor to face us. "I told you that he'd probably be in the cafeteria. That's the only place around here where they haven't started parking stretchers."

Seeing that there was no place for both of us either to stand or sit, Sam begged off for a minute to check his incoming messages. We both watched his white coat-tails fly down the hall.

"Well, what do you think of your big brother, Mr Cooperman? He's something else all right." I agreed with her. Here at the hospital, Sam was fully grown up. Outside, when I saw him at weddings and funerals, he seemed like a kid trying out his father's clothes.

"I like what I see, Ms Levine." Although I'd talked to her earlier, I was feeling shy all over again. Shyness brings out the formal in me. "And thank you for all the help you've been to me already. And to Sam."

"Don't get me all choked up, hon. And you better call me 'Monica,' lest I forget you're talking to me."

"Just the same, it's not easy making your way in a hostile environment."

"He's doing okay. He's got good instincts: knows how to get by the barracudas."

"You think one of them got to Dr Horner?"

"Davidson Horner? Hell, he eats barracuda for lunch. He's just gone fishing, I expect. Never did worry much about holding up his hand and asking to leave the room. It's like going on general rounds with him. He starts when he's ready. He doesn't wait around for late-comers, just moves ahead like a cold front moving in off the ocean."

"I'm beginning to form a picture of Dr Horner. Was he likable?"

"Always a perfect gentleman with me. My colour kept him on his best behaviour. He was never fully relaxed. But you go talk to Irene, his secretary. She knew him better than anybody. I've already had a wee word in her ear, so she's expecting you. I told her not to hold back."

"I'll do that. Thanks." We talked for another minute or two. She told me that she grew up in Moncton, and then lived in Montreal. Emboldened by her frankness, I asked, "May I ask you how you got your last name?"

"You're a curious cat for a little fellow, aren't you? Sam wondered about that too. There used to be a Dr Alan Levine in my life. Now I'm putting our two kids through school."

"And Dr Levine? Sorry, I know it's none –"

"The good doctor's in a home getting better care than I could give him. He got one of those nasty diseases that affect the nerve endings. Gives him terrible pain all of the time; can't stand anything touching him. It's got to the point where he's tired of being alive. Everything's a burden to him, poor lamb."

"I'm sorry."

"Uh huh, me too. He's too good a man to lose like this."

Monica gave me a choice from a box of chocolates, imported from Riga, Latvia. Best I ever tasted. "They're some good, aren't they? Friend brought them back from a visit. Take another." I did.

By the time I was beginning to feel like I was standing in the way of her getting on with her work, Sam was back.

"Why don't you two go off and look for Dr Horner in the laundry or the kitchens, and let me finish reading this directive on applications for special leave. It's so fascinating, you wouldn't believe it."

I followed Sam down the corridor, which was lined with gurneys, some with ivs on stands and some without. I was surprised that the crowding even invaded the corridors of power. He led me around three corners, a step up into an older part of the building, and finally to an office door somewhat larger than his own. It looked like it had been taken out of an old bank building being demolished and inserted here on the whim of someone with enough power to make it stick. Sam knocked. Almost at once, the portal was opened by someone who could never have been Irene Uhrynuk.

"Samuel!" the stranger said, the formality intended as humorous, with an edge of irony. He was a big man with shoulders that tried to mask his tallness. This resulted in making him appear to have a hollow chest, which wasn't the case at all. He tried out a grin on the two of us, not a whole-hearted grin, but one that remembered the seriousness of the times. It was both affable and a call to duty.

"Oh, hi, Clive." I tried to remember who Clive was. I should have written this stuff down in my head instead of on the clipboard now safe in Sam's cupboard. "Clive, I want you to meet my brother Ben from Grantham. He's in town for a couple of days. Benny, this is Dr Bardell." He stuck out his hand and I took it. His was a minimal squeeze, suitable for visiting firemen; he was saving his good ones for the power elite.

"How are you?" he asked, and while I started to mumble something, he continued: "Getting the Cook's tour of Sam's new empire, are you? Maybe he'll let you watch an appendectomy in the operating theatre with the medical students. This is a busy teaching hospital, you know."

"I seem to have timed my visit badly," I said, trying to get the banter stopped. "You've got some sort of crisis at the hospital."

"The normal work still goes on," he said. "We can't shut down to retool whenever a crisis hits. Nowadays we live from crisis to crisis. You never know what the morrow will bring. Nice to meet you, ah, Mr Cooperman."

53

"Are you a surgeon, Dr Bardell?"

"Not on your life. I'm a researcher. Special project and all that. I have my glory hole on the sixth floor. You must come and have a look while you're here. You can see more than eyelashes through a microscope."

"I'd like that," I said, as Dr Bardell moved off down the hall at a fast pace. "Is he always in a hurry?" I asked.

"We're all in a hurry, Benny. We're short staffed, overworked and underfunded." Sam held the door so I could enter Horner's office. I did so thinking that if money was tight, the research boys are probably feeling the pinch the hardest. No wonder Bardell took off at such a trot.

Inside the door, Irene Uhrynuk sat at her computer. She gave Sam a friendly smile, with just a touch of world-weariness around the edges.

"Hello, Sam," she said with a shade of Ava Gardner in Mogambo. Her voice had sultry fires backed up inside, while the exterior was all business and efficiency.

"Irene, this is my brother Benny. I told you that he was going to be in town for a couple of days."

Irene Uhrynuk got up at once and held out a friendly hand. She was about fifty, with good bones in her face and grey hair worn in a style of a bygone season. She was wearing a crisp blouse with a navy sweater and was as buxom as a cheerleader. I could imagine that she had been wearing some version of this outfit for the past thirty years or more.

"I'm very glad to meet you, Benny. Sam has been telling me about your adventures since he came here. How exciting to be a private detective!"

"Not so loud, Irene. Around here, Benny's just another tourist. The less anyone knows about him, the better." Irene mimed the locking of her mouth and hiding the key between her breasts.

"Irene, I promised Benny that you would be able to give him a few minutes."

"Sure. Glad to help. We are all puzzled by Dr Horner's sudden disappearance." Sam begged off, and Irene Uhrynuk led me into Dr

Horner's *sanctum sanctorum*.

Now this was everybody's idea of what a doctor's office should be. There were books from floor to ceiling on four walls, windows on two sides, and paintings, portraits mostly, above leather-covered stuffed chairs and sofas. There was a scattering of bell jars with things inside I didn't want to see too closely, floating in formaldehyde like weightless astronauts. Irene took a chair and I sat myself down in another. The chair farted as it took up my weight.

"Where to begin?" she said, then added, "Monica said I should open up to you. I like Monica's instincts about people."

"Sam has sketched out the broad outline of Dr Horner's life, but what I need are your intuitions, based on your unique knowledge of the man. You know I'm not just a curious stranger; I hope to be able to help find him. Anything you tell me will remain confidential unless it turns out to be the key to his disappearance. I'm not here in Toronto looking for sensational disclosures. But sometimes they lead right to where we want to go."

"Sure. I understand."

"Was there a deep, dark secret that might be behind this?"

"Oh, Dr Horner was a lot of things, but never a man of mystery. His habits were regular and his pleasures few and above board. There were no floozies on the side, no hidden life, no picture of Dorian Gray hidden in the old school room."

"Well, that's a start. What about his working on the weekend?"

"What about it? Dr Horner worked when there was work to be done. He didn't keep to a nine-to-five schedule and didn't expect others to either. A good deal of my job was trying to make the doctor understand that people had families, made commitments, and were not hanging around suspended in some hospital blue room waiting to be summoned to this office. Since he had no life beyond this hospital, he had difficulty taking people seriously whose dedication did not match his own."

"What was he like to work for? It must have been like a war zone in here at times."

"We knew each other, Benny. He knew when my plate was full and I tried to translate the early twenty-first century to him. He was missing that bump in the head that gives some people the social graces. But he made do."

"Good. Had you noticed any break in the pattern recently? Anything out of the way? Uncharacteristic behaviour?"

"When I saw him last on Friday at about six, he was the same man who hired me thirty years ago when I was eighteen."

"You've been very loyal."

"He could be a crotchety, stubborn old man at times. He could be a proper tyrant, he could out-herod Herod, but he always remembered my birthday."

"Remarkable man."

"Yes, he was." Having said that, her hand flew to her mouth. "Is, I mean. Most definitely, is."

"And yet, somewhere, you've entertained the thought that ..."

"I wouldn't say entertained. It occurred to me, that's all; as a possibility, as a remote possibility."

"Yes."

"Benny, you must understand that talking about Dr Horner is like talking about a force of nature. He is that. Every inch of him. Look at his portrait over there." She indicated one of the portraits against the wooden panelling.

"Is that Dr Horner? I never saw him."

"That's the Barker Fairley portrait. There are two others hanging elsewhere in the building. There's another in the school of medicine."

I moved over to look at the face looking out at me. It was a big, meaty face, with deep-set, penetrating eyes, monumental brows. It was a powerful face, like a sculptured head. There was something electrifying about it, something magisterial.

"Is it a good likeness?" I asked turning back to Irene.

"Barker always tried to catch more than just a likeness. At times, I think it is him."

I returned to my chair. Once again it passed wind under me.

"Tell me about his health," I asked, trying to free myself from looking back at the picture.

"Oh, he has a spring cold, regular as clockwork. Flu about five

56

times in ten years. No serious ailments that I know about."

"Who's his doctor?"

"Blostein. One of the Blostein brothers. H. P., not B. E. But you won't get anything out of Henry. The police can't and you won't."

"I can live with that."

Irene gave me a straight look, like she was still trying to measure me for an opinion.

"Have you been worrying about him, Irene?"

"He's got his sister to look out for him. I just run the office. If you want to know whether he wears a truss or not, you'd better ask Plum."

"Plum?"

"That's his sister. She's in the German Department over at the university. Her name started out as Penelope, then it was shortened to Penny, and now it's Plum. She keeps house for him. Neither one ever married. They're the end of their line."

"You don't like Plum much, do you?"

"What's there for me to like or dislike? She doesn't visit him here. I don't see him away from the hospital. I've never heard a word spoken against the woman."

I thought it might be smart to shift the conversation away from Horner's sister. "Why do the people around here have it in for Sam?"

"Oh! You have to have a reason, do you? Sam's a fine doctor and he'll do well here. He's simply the victim of some initiation hazing."

"There's something more than that, Irene."

"Well, yes, there is. Some of the staff resent the irregular manner of his coming here. Put it down to professional jealousy. Senior medical men can be as childish as children, Benny. They'll get over it. All of the knives aimed at his back aren't made of steel. Most are rubber."

"I see," I said, relieved a little.

"You have to understand, Benny, that a hospital is a mediæval institution. There's nothing modern about it. Oh, they have people who dress it up in the language of the day. They write "he or she" in their public-relations press releases, pay lip service to political correctness and gender equality. Dr Galt sees to that when it's an outside communication. But this is as much a man's world today as it was in the time of Lister or Ostler. Don't let them fool you."

"I guess you would know." I was beginning to suspect that this wasn't Kansas anymore. For some reason, that reminded me of a question I meant to ask her. "Tell me, Irene, was Horner – excuse me, Dr Horner – worried about anything that you know about, either officially or unofficially?"

"He was an obsessive type, Benny. Once he got a bee in his bonnet he'd be hell to live with until he got rid of it. Like this prostate thing."

"What prostate thing?"

"Oh, damn! I was told not to mention that to anybody."

"Who told you to sit on it?"

"I shouldn't be telling you this."

"Yes, you should. It might help find him. Who told you not to say anything?"

"Mr O'Donahue and Dr Bardell. I wanted to tell Inspector Salter, but Dr Bardell was standing right there being helpful. I couldn't say a word. Dr Bardell said it was bad security to talk about that to the police so soon. If he's still away next week, he says, we can take another look."

"Why does Dr Bardell loom so large in the scheme of things? I thought he was a humble researcher."

"He's a top researcher, Benny. He has a big budget. His team isolated HIV (Beta) six years ago."

"I still don't see why he's standing shoulder to shoulder with Mr O'Donahue in inventing policy to cover Dr Horner's unexplained absence."

"Well, if you must know, Benny, Dr Bardell was one of Dr Horner's protégés."

"You mean one of the students he'd taken under his wing?"

"Yes, that's true, but there was more."

"Horner found a place for him like he'd done for others who struck his fancy."

"Right, but it was even closer than that, I think. He's always taken an almost fatherly interest in Clive." I took a minute to digest this bit of news. When I'd caught my breath, I asked the question I'd been holding onto since Irene first mentioned it.

"Now, tell me about this prostate thing. Was he worried about his?"

"Aren't most men of his age? He'd been making some furtive calls to a doctor in Winnipeg. Prostate specialist. He was away three weeks ago for two days in Winnipeg."

"But why Winnipeg? Do they have a new treatment or something?"

"No, of course not. But Dr Horner's a very private man. He wouldn't have his tonsils out under this roof just in case anybody asked whether he was admitted properly and so on. Another thing: I think he's shy about his personal health. He wouldn't want to take his shirt off in front of any of the junior staff."

"What's the name of the Winnipeg doctor, Irene?"

"David Grierson of the Fort Garry General."

"What is his specialty?"

"Prostate cancer, Benny. He's the best man in the world for prostate cancer."

— NINE —

The offices of Denbigh Publishing were on Richmond Street near Spadina Avenue; they occupied half a floor of an old dry goods warehouse that had been refashioned into studios and showrooms. Salter heard Vera Denbigh's voice from along the corridor and followed the sound to an open door through which he saw her, sitting behind a desk, grinning, waiting for a reply to her shouted instruction to "send him to Saskatoon." The answer came back, "By train?"

"Buy him a bus ticket." Now she focused on Salter, standing in the doorway. "Oh, God. Are you an author?" she demanded. "No? Good. I've spoken to three authors this morning. That's my quota. What can I do for you?"

Salter explained himself.

"Oh boy," she said. "Oh boy, oh boy, oh boy," She shook herself. "Sorry, I was thinking of something else. So Dr Horner's gone missing, has he? What do you want me to say? Prepare yourself for the worst."

"Huh?"

"Because I cannot imagine Horner running away with his secretary, and therefore for him to disappear could be bad. Perhaps he has been in an accident. Come in and shut the door. Have a seat."

"I think we would have heard," Salter said, taking the chair opposite her. "He's been missing for a couple of days."

"Alzheimer's?"

"Did you ever see any signs of it?"

"No. Perhaps he did have a secret life." She said it as if they were sharing a small joke.

"He lives with his sister. She said there were no gaps in his routines."

"Sounds bad. So find his enemies."

"I'm looking. Did he have any in that book club you both belong to?"

"You mean the Boswell Club? It's not a book club. Just a lunchtime gabfest of book people."

"What was he doing in a group like that?"

"I brought him in." She had lowered her voice, comically, not wanting the information to get out. Then, returning to normal," We are both on the board of Rose of Sharon Hospital." She stopped to consider what she was going to say. "He never said much."

"Why are you on the hospital board?"

"What's that got to do with you?"

"Nothing. Just curious." He thought of something. "My wife might ask me. She's interested in what it takes to be a prominent woman, a mover and shaker."

She laughed. "Rude bugger, aren't you? I'm the token lay member – the woman, the outsider. At any one time you'll find me on the board of something, or on a committee advising somebody. I don't do the symphony or art gallery, but I get tapped for everything else."

"The Police Board?"

"I'll give it a turn. Ask me."

"Horner is there officially, of course."

"I assume so. He never confided in me until one day he realized who I was, or what I was, more like, and he got that gleam in his eye and I knew he was going to proposition me with a manuscript."

"That happen often?"

"Oh God, no. Not you, too."

Salter laughed. "You get a lot of people coming at you with manuscripts?"

"When you see that gleam you can only hope it means he is going to put his hand on your leg, show you his etchings, but it always turns out to be a manuscript he wants to show you."

"Must be hell."

"Usually I see it coming and refer them to my editorial department. That's Sally."

"What kind of books do these strangers write?"

"Mysteries and memoirs," she said promptly. "Everyone has one of each in a drawer waiting for a sucker like me to reveal what I do. You don't have one, do you?"

"Don't worry. So which did Horner have?"

"Now we are coming to it. He is writing a history of Rose of Sharon where he has worked for most of his professional life. It isn't very promising."

"Dull?"

"Is that door closed? At the moment it is five hundred and fifty pages of single-space foolscap typing. I estimate about a thousand words a page, which comes to about half a million words. No sex, no violence, just chat. It's called *A Doctor Remembers*.

"What are you going to do with it?"

"I don't know yet."

"Why did you invite him into your – gabfest?"

"I invited him as a guest in the first place, because I could never publish his manuscript, and I thought I should be nice to him personally if not to his manuscript. And he was thrilled, so much so that he asked me to put him up for membership. And then by one of those acts of fate, George Dragwater, the writer who..."

"I know who George Dragwater is."

"Sorry. Of course, everyone knows George. Well, George was in our hospital having his kidneys checked or some such and I mentioned to Dr Horner that he was one of the people he'd met around our table and he promptly visited George and asked him, too, to put him up for membership, and he did. George told me afterwards that he's frightened of dying and he thought the nurses would look after him better if they saw how friendly he was with the chief of staff. So there it was. Horner was proposed, and no one objected. That was my job and I funked it. He's been a faithful member for a year now."

"Fits right in, does he?"

"He's a bump on a log. But enough. What else do you want to know? He doesn't have any enemies around the table, I can tell you that. The hospital is more likely."

"Why?"

"Because he holds most of his medical colleagues in contempt, genial contempt, some of them, and some of them – what is the word? I don't know, just contempt. Disdain, that's the word. And they are wary of the rumours of what's in his memoir, as they should

"Oh, God. Are you an author?" she demanded.

be. If it were well written, interesting, and an important social document, I still couldn't publish it because there is a libel or character assassination on every other page. Maybe every third page. All the way from the students he was in medical school with on throughout his career, including most of the staff and present administration of Rose of Sharon. My God, even I'm in it: he calls me Rose of Sharon's Zsa Zsa. He doesn't think I might be offended. I'm not even Hungarian, for God's sake. So you see, if anyone else has seen this manuscript, he might have a *lot* of enemies. My impression is that a number of people know about it and would like to get their hands on a copy."

"Surely he would know he couldn't print stuff like that? Did you talk to him about it? That would be the way you could get out of publishing it, wouldn't it?"

"Of course, but he said there would be no problem. He hadn't identified anybody, you see, cleverly calling them all Dr X or Nurse Y, or The Anæsthetist. But all the other details are there – dates, times, places, so it isn't hard to penetrate his disguises. Even I knew a couple of them from my work on the board. You know what? *I'm* your chief suspect, if you are looking for one." She grinned.

"Someone has told me off the record that although he's very successful, he isn't or wasn't actually a brilliant doctor. He must have some idea of that. So why is he contemptuous of his colleagues?"

"You're right. Not for their medical knowledge. But Horner is one of those people who make a fetish of knowing grammar. He is always making a fuss if you confuse 'disinterested' with 'uninterested' or 'which' with 'that.' His *bête noir* is the use of adverbs instead of adjectives after copula verbs, as in, 'I feel well' or 'more importantly' instead of 'more important' implying the silent 'is.' He didn't do it to me because English is my second language, so I know the rules better than he does. But he couldn't resist correcting his colleagues. His favourite question was to ask when you use a capital after a colon, and when a lower case. Do you know?"

"No."

"Horner does."

"Can I see the manuscript?"

"I'm sorry to tell you, Inspector, that we can't find it. I decided the manuscript ought to be put away somewhere safe until I had another talk with Horner, and I asked my assistant, Sally, to keep it locked up, but she didn't have it. She said she was still waiting for me to give it to her, so we did a search. Nothing. Publishers do lose manuscripts occasionally, but usually before we've read them. Authors come in to ask when they might hear about the manuscript they submitted six months ago and it's the first we've heard of it. In this case, as you see, I remember it clearly, but at some point in the last three months it has vanished."

"Do you keep manuscripts locked up?"

"Of course not. We don't even lock our offices. Sometimes in special cases, we might lock a script in a drawer, though I can't remember the last time I did that. I'm certain I didn't lock *A Doctor Remembers* away anywhere. Why would I? I didn't find it precious. Valuable, I mean."

"Do you remember when you last saw it?"

"When Horner came in to talk to me about it. We sort of handled the manuscript as I told him about our concern."

"Do you remember how the interview ended? Who else was around?"

"I think you're wasting your time on that one. The one or two people who looked at it found it excruciatingly dull, in spite of the libellous content. I told you how it was written, didn't I? It was all 'and then.' Every paragraph contained at least one 'and then,' sometimes two."

"Would you do another search for me, now?"

"This minute?"

"Today."

Then, for Salter's benefit, she became Czech again, at least central European, digging her fingers into the hair hanging down on each side of her face, flinging it up, banging her elbows on the table, and shouting, "Goddamn Davidson Horner. I wish he would walk in that door and I could find his manuscript and tell him what to do with it." But he didn't, so she couldn't, and Salter left after reminding her that he'd like to get the result of the search that afternoon.

An hour later Vera Denbigh called Salter at the hospital where he was using Horner's office. "The mystery is solved," she shouted. "You hear? The mystery is solved! One of my editors, Patrick, remembered and will swear on oath that he was standing in the doorway when Horner was leaving, and he saw him put the manuscript in his briefcase."

"But Horner has the original."

"Of course. But both of us must have forgotten that we were looking at my copy, so when we finished, he packed it away in his bag. It was probably a Freudian oversight on my part. I was so glad to be rid of it."

"And on his part?"

"That, too, would be the behaviour of your average anal-retentive. He couldn't resist tidying my desk." She laughed, a huge cackling laugh. "The mystery is solved," she repeated.

TEN

I was suffering from information overload. I'd learned too much too soon and I was about to start losing it unless I could put it into some frame or other. Irene told me where the library was on the second floor. It wasn't as big as a real library, but it appeared to be up to date on all of the cusps of medical practice today. I found myself a table in the back near a window overlooking a street of Chinese restaurants.

First I headed for *Who's Who* and looked up "Horner, John Davidson."

Horner, John Davidson, O.C., B.Sc. (Med.) M.D., F.R.C.P.(C), F.A.C.P., F.R.S.C., LL.D, D.U. ; medical doctor, hospital administrator, educator; b. Toronto, Ont. 20 Aug. 1938; s. Alexander Prescott and Agnes (McPhee) H.; e. Upper Canada College, Toronto 1956 (Nesbitt Gold Medal); Univ. Coll., Univ. of Toronto; M.D. Univ. of Toronto, 1960; Ph.D. Johns Hopkins, 1962; ...

And so it went, on and on, with prizes and medals at every turn. No listed wives, sisters, or children. Just honour after honour with boards of directorships and trusteeships at Baden Baden and Karachi. Recreations were listed as reading and writing. No summer address. It was a list that only the subject would have patience to read all the way through. All very interesting, if you enjoy that sort of thing.

O'Donahue had a modest entry. He's been on the hospital board since 1995. He was "a member of Rotary (past Pres.); Kinsmen (Life Member); K. of C. (Past Grand Kt.)..." It listed him as a Conservative. Why wasn't I surprised?

There was no entry for Clive Bardell in *Who's Who*. He hadn't earned it yet, but a smaller biographical tome, dedicated to the profession of medicine, listed Dr Clive Russell Bardell in the right place.

He was forty-two, his recreations were listed as swimming, back-packing, and bird-watching. He belonged to an array of prestigious clubs located on University Avenue and out in the boondocks. There was no mention of his parentage, and I wondered if he had dropped them off, now that he was successful. It happens. His wife was the former Audrey Farrar. No children. I tried the name Farrar in the big *Who's Who*. It had a Farrar, Joseph Reid, who claimed a daughter, Audrey. Joseph Reid Farrar was a professor of anatomy, a department head no less, at the University of Toronto. He was born in Round Hill, Ontario. In the big atlas I found Round Hill just north of Mount Forest, in southern Ontario's farming country.

If I'd met a few more of Horner's colleagues, I could have looked them up too. I scouted in the fat books for Galt, Francis; Morgan, Ivor; and Hui, Paul, without becoming much wiser. They all played racquetball. Maybe it was a conspiracy to get a court installed at the hospital and Horner was blocking it. I knew I'd figure it out if I only gave it time enough. On the library shelves, I found a few monographs by Horner on various topics; the early ones were on medical topics and the more recent ones were about medical policy and hospital administration. There was a fat brief to the Ontario government about the proper inspection of drinking water, written in conjunction with public health officials. Dr Bardell had a few slim booklets himself, in the row between Banting and Best. He seemed to be obsessed with the prostate gland and its functions and malfunctions. The back of the book described him as the chairman of the Munn Research Project. When I looked up Munn, I discovered a family of three sisters who were underwriting worthy medical projects with inherited money.

To fill in the time before lunch – I was feeling peckish – I wrote down some of the information I'd been looking at: hometowns, clubs, medical schools.

From the library I started back to Sam's office. Near his door a security guard collared me. He was older than the people I saw downstairs in the Emergency Room, and he looked more like a cop than most of them do. "It's Mr Cooperman, right?"

"That's right. What can I do for you?"

"Would you kindly come with me?"

"Maybe. If you tell me why."

"My supervisor would like a word with you. He's just behind the information booth in the main floor lobby."

"What's his name, your supervisor?"

"You mean Mr Prinsep? Val Prinsep. He's been chief here for five years or more."

I followed the guard along the colour-coded corridor and down the elevator – I forget the colour – to the guard room, which was fitted into one of the rounded walls of the lobby. It was a leftover bit of space intended to draw people towards the information desk, which was at the centre of a circle described by the walls. Inside, the space had been adapted to hold a board full of clusters of keys, a duty schedule, and a time clock. Prinsep had a smallish desk in a corner. He was a thick-set, sallow man with a moustache that looked like it was fastened with spirit gum. There were humourous wrinkles around his eyes. When he saw me, he got to his feet and stretched a friendly hand across the litter on his desk.

"Mr Cooperman! Glad you could make it. Sit down." He cleared a shoebox of paper off the seat of a folding chair and dusted it off playfully. Other files were kept in red and blue plastic milk crates.

"I'd feel better about this if I knew what it was all about."

"Would you like some tea or coffee?" he asked.

"Thanks, no. I'd settle for an explanation."

"We've been on the lookout for you, Mr Cooperman. We knew you'd been in the building and asking questions."

"Anything wrong with that? I'm a licenced private investigator, hired by a senior staff member who has been questioned by the police about the disappearance of your CEO. I'm here by invitation."

"Don't lose your cool, Mr Cooperman. I just wanted you to know where to find us. We're around the hospital twenty-four hours a day. Mostly these days, we're trying to keep order in Emerg. But our interest stretches to all thirteen floors and two basements."

"So, you don't have a problem with me being here?"

"If you can stand it, we can. We're all worried about Dr Horner."

"You think that Dr Horner's in the building?"

"We've been into every closet and cupboard. We've checked elevator shafts, the roof, air shafts, and the whole maze of boiler rooms and furnaces. We've even been into the air vents and crawl spaces. Nothing. And we've looked in every room, both in the active part of the hospital and in the closed-off sections."

"'Closed-off sections'? Is that because of lack of funding?"

"Yeah, they cut off so many beds and then pretend they don't exist, because there's no staff to service them. Doc Horner's not in any of those cut-off rooms. Not even under the beds."

"How did you know I was here?"

"Mr Cooperman, I heard about the way you treated that bastard across the street at NTV a few months ago. After that, you can have anything from me. Their security head was getting money on the side from every crook in town. He gave us all a black eye."

"Doesn't answer the question."

"It wasn't intended to."

I smiled across the desk at Prinsep and backed away. There wasn't room to leave any other way. I caught another glimpse of the chaos spilling my way from the Emergency room, and pushed the nearest elevator button.

Monica told me that Sam was away from his desk. That's one of those phrases that can cover anything from a short trip to the bathroom to a summer ramble in the Pyrenees. I asked her what she could tell me about Clive Bardell, but she didn't add much to what I'd just been reading. I told her that I was going out to lunch. She approved the idea, but declined the invitation to join me, nodding her head at the pile of work in front of her. I followed a couple of interns out a back door and ended up at a big round table shared with a Chinese family, in a restaurant on Baldwin Street called Kowloon. I watched what they ordered and simply pointed at their dishes when the waitress showed some interest in my appetite. I'd been to Kowloon before, on an earlier trip to Toronto, and recognized the husband of the manager, who looked like a Chinese Charles Bronson. I ate happily for some time. So did the interns, who were enjoying dim sum selections, which I had trouble sorting out on my own.

I didn't return to the hospital directly. A detour through the big

City Hall (there was nothing like that in Grantham) brought me to the registry office. Here I applied for a birth notice of Clive Russell Bardell. I filled out the forms and gave an address where the material could be sent. When I requested a rush be put on the order, I got a lecture that they rush all of their orders through as fast as possible. The manager himself told me that there would be no "jumping the queue" while he was in charge. A woman at the next window slipped me a wink. Ten minutes later, I returned to her window and got what I was after – for the usual nominal fee. While I was at City Hall, I did my share of rubber-necking, looked at a scale model of downtown Toronto, found the Rose of Sharon in its proper place, and returned to the sunlight feeling as though I had been pushing some of the right buttons.

When I looked at the form, the original dating back to 1959, I could see that the information was incomplete and sketchy. The place of birth was given as Round Hill, Ontario. That was the sort of place I organize in my head under the heading "Up North." No father was mentioned. Somehow, I wasn't surprised by that. No mother either. No wonder Horner looked after him like a son. Horner was as close to a father as Bardell got. Maybe he was Horner's wild oat? An embarrassing flaw in that well-armoured, selfless rectitude, as my friend Frank Bushmill, a medical man himself, might have put it. It was a funny thought, like finding out that William Lyon Mackenzie, the backbone of the 1837 Rebellion in Upper Canada, whose face was in all of my school books, had a bastard son. Highly embarrassing for the school system, in the same way that they went on publishing stories by Oscar Wilde, but forgot to put his name on them. Probably forgot to send royalties to his publisher too. It showed amoral and political sensitivity that didn't lose them any money.

The paper in my hand was curious from another point of view: there was a delay of some weeks between the date of birth and the date of registration. Usually, the dates are only days apart; here, I counted two and a half months.

There is a library at City Hall – not a reference library, but a neighbourhood circulating branch of the Toronto system. I sat down in a corner, surrounded by Allingham, Christie, and Doyle. Hill, Innes, and James were on the next shelf. Mason, Parker, and Poe were behind me. It felt comfortable to have so much talent at my elbow, even if it was fictional. I pulled down a copy of Poe's stories. I'd been given a copy, nicely bound in blue leather, when I was twelve. I still remember the delight with which I devoured each of the stories. It was while I was looking at the Table of Contents that it came to me. In the case of "The Purloined Letter," Dupin figures out how to find a document that has so far eluded all of his skill. In the end, he finds that the missing letter was hidden all the time in plain view, exactly where nobody'd think of looking for it. That's how I began to suspect where Horner might be.

ELEVEN

Keen to get a look at Horner's manuscript, Salter waylaid his sister in her office at the university.

"The manuscript will be at home in Davidson's briefcase," she said in response to his request. "I've got to finish this report before I go home. If you can come back in an hour, we'll go there together, and I'll give it to you. Tell you what, why don't we take the opportunity to walk one of the trails, follow Davidson home, as it were. All right? I'd like the exercise. In an hour, then."

It wasn't, Salter thought, that she was in the least like Margaret Rutherford; he just thought he understood better now how actors like Margaret Rutherford invented themselves out of pieces of the people they met. In Plum Horner's case, it was the absence of any "ers" or "ums" in her speech, the crisp clarity of the brief sentences, that reminded him of Madame Arcarti.

She nodded to dismiss him and went back to her computer.

* * *

An hour later they set off for the hospital, to begin the walk to the subway station on Yonge Street.

"So far, you see, broad daylight, open fields, no chance of ambush. Now, over here…" She took his arm and led him down into the subway station.

"Token?" she asked. "Never mind." She dropped two tokens into the box and led him to the escalator.

The train was packed and Salter put a little space between them, so she would not be tempted into conversation in a voice that would cut through the susurrations of the other commuters; her voice was not loud, but it had an edge that would engrave itself on the hubbub with ease. Once, Salter had bumped into an academic he knew slightly on the same train, an English professor whom he had interviewed previously about a colleague who was murdered. The professor greeted him immediately in his lecturing voice, hard, bright, and easily projecting to the back of Convocation Hall or a subway car. He regaled Salter with a story of how he had once, on the Paris Metro, been jammed between three prostitutes who started to proposition him, offering him a session, competing with each other on price, teasing him, he realized, while he tried to explain to them that he was on the way to the cinema. Mixed up in the story, or illustrating it, was another story about a Browning poem that had to do, according to the professor, with the *argot* for sanitary napkins. All this in a voice like a lot of plates breaking, punctuated with the hisses and gurgles of the speaker's enjoyment of his own story. Salter had made up his mind to get off and catch the next train, but the academic left instead, leaving Salter with a carriage full of commuters staring at him intently. Thus he leaned away from Plum Horner, just in case, until they reached Summerhill, their stop.

"He might have gone to the liquor store," she said, gesturing to their left as they walked out to Yonge Street. "But there was no need. Better assume not. In any case, he would have crossed at the traffic light – here we go." She took his arm again and they walked north. "People knew him," she said. "His barber, Keith Miller, the dry-cleaner, the mini mart. You may want to check on them. I already have, of course. Here we are, Woodlawn. You see, not a dark alley or sinister wood to be seen the whole way."

Inside the house, sweetly scented with lavender or some such, she waved her hand around the first floor. "This is our communal space," she said. "Here I cook and we eat and, when absolutely necessary, entertain jointly, though we try not to do a lot of that. Out here," she led him through a glass door on to the deck behind the house, "is Davidson's garden. Look at it. He really should have been a gardener, or a literary person. He never really had a taste for medicine, if I can make a play on words, and he's glad to be away from the hands-on stuff."

Salter looked around while she was talking, taking in the elaborate rock garden, still multi-coloured even in September, the ornamental pool with the ancient gnome in the centre holding a stone carp, standing on a mushroom of rock. "That was in our garden when we were children, and we managed to hook it when Mother went. Trendy people have been sneering at gnomes for about fifty years, and now they're fashionable again, especially authentic stone ones, like Rupert there." She led him back inside. "Let's go upstairs. The second floor is mine and the third is Davidson's."

Each floor consisted of a bedroom, an elaborate bathroom, a sitting room/study, and a spare room. "We don't often have guests at the same time," she said. "But we can. We have cousins in Vancouver whom I encourage to visit once a year for a night or two, and now I get the odd grown-up child. Davidson is indifferent, but I like the idea of family. Now here we have his study. First, let's get the briefcase. It's a horrible goat-sick yellow that's an epithet from our childhood; we used to compete in creating disgusting imagery – made of pigskin with straps."

They circled the room, opening drawers and cabinets. Salter checked under the bed, in the closets, pulling furniture away from the walls. There was no sign of the briefcase. There was nowhere to store such a thing in the bathroom; the hall linen closet contained only towels and sheets.

"Where do you send your laundry?" Salter asked, pointing to the beautifully laundered linen, not only perfectly ironed and folded but wrapped in pairs in white drawing-paper tied close with a piece of wide blue tape secured with a neat bow. "That's his work," she said. "His hobby. He doesn't cook, but he does everything else, including the laundry and the sewing. I cook. Now, have we looked everywhere? Wait a minute, I forgot this." She reached down to the bottom shelf of a metal trolley, which carried, on its surface, a Webster's dictionary, and lifted up a large brown paper parcel. "Here we are."

She unwrapped the brown paper and lifted out the top sheet of script, a list of page numbers with one-word references, apparently pointing to changes required in the manuscript. Next came the cover, *A Doctor Remembers* label pasted on a sheet of thin red cardboard; then came the manuscript proper, perhaps four inches thick.

About two weeks' reading.

"There we are," she said. "End of quest."

"I don't think so," Salter said. "This isn't the one. This is too clean."

"Of course. You're quite right. This is his own copy. It never left the house. So we are nowhere."

"Yes, we are. You saw the other copy in his briefcase?"

"I was here when he brought it home last week. I never saw it leave, but I never saw Davidson go to the hospital without his brief-case, because he wouldn't eat the cafeteria food, so I made him a sandwich every day or he bought one at a delicatessen. He carried it in his briefcase. So unless the copy we are looking for is hidden very carefully, then it is in his office, probably still in the briefcase."

"Can I borrow the copy?"

"I suppose so. It should be safe with you, shouldn't it?"

TWELVE

"Who's the hospital expert on Dr Bardell?" I wondered out loud, while chatting with Irene Uhrynuk and Monica Levine late the following morning.

Irene and Monica pointed at one another.

"Thanks a lot," I said, with heavy sarcasm.

"Why your interest in Dr Bardell, Mr C?"

"I'm not so much interested in Bardell as I am in Dr Horner's interest in him. Am I right in thinking that Bardell is more than one of Horner's protégés?"

"I'm sure you're right," Monica chimed in. "Without Horner, there'd be no Bardell. At least, not here."

"The only thing I know for sure about Dr Bardell," said Monica, with a sly smile, "is that he has a reputation as the slowest credit card in the whole hospital. He'd rather eat free than eat at all. It's his nature."

"Still, it's likely that Bardell might know something about Horner that no one else does, something private."

At ten minutes to twelve, Dr Clive Bardell came out of the boardroom on the third floor, whither I'd been sent by my two informants. There was a small wager riding on whether I could interest Bardell in my treating him to lunch. He approached two or three colleagues as he moved through the corridor; all of them shook their heads and hurried on. He caught sight of me standing there, smiling at the brickwork I could see through a dusty window, and approached me with a smile. "Those meetings are getting to run longer every month. Makes a man hungry as the sun stands above the steeple. How are you, Mr Cooperman?"

"Not bad, nothing serious, nothing a good meal can't fix."

"Say, if you're in an eating frame of mind, I can show you a great place to have dim sum."

"Great! And it will give me a chance to quiz you about Dr Horner."

"It's a done deal, then. Come on." I followed Bardell back to the elevator bank and through a side door that led out the Elm Street side, past the Golgotha of Emerg, with its groaning humanity.

Maybe you don't know it, but there's a good Chinese restaurant on Chestnut Street. It's on the mezzanine floor of a new hotel. The day that Bardell and I walked in, half the tables were occupied by lawyers and judges, some of them still in their black robes, and all still wearing their starched tabs. I felt a little underdressed in a sports coat and mismatched pants. We were seated at a round table with a white tablecloth and served tea before asking for it from white tea service. I let Bardell order. He knew the menu by heart, filling out the red-printed order sheet with dispatch. He waved at a couple of our fellow diners, one a lovely, dark-haired beauty wearing attractive glasses. She waved back, but neither bothered to get up.

"She used to work in the Prime Minister's office," Bardell said over our teacups. I looked again, watching her engage her companion in animated talk. I was wondering, while I watched her, how to drag animated talk from my companion. This meal would go on my expenses, if Monica Levine is a good judge of character. I didn't mind that – Sam could afford it – but I was hungry for information as well as for my lunch.

"I always envy people who know where the best places lie, off the beaten track, not the usual tourist places. In Toronto, I've always been a tourist. I usually eat on Yonge Street or Bloor." I hoped that that might be a big enough bone to get him started.

"Is that a fact, Mr Cooperman? You should get Sam to show you the town."

"I should, but I don't think I'll be here much longer. I'm just a small-town boy; I don't follow big-city police procedures. I'll quietly go back to my skip-tracing and divorce work. And little enough of that there is nowadays." I hoped I wasn't laying it on too thick.

"It's a shame you weren't able to help out a little more."

"How does Dr Horner's disappearance affect you, doctor? Beyond the loss of an old friend and colleague, I mean."

"He was that and more, Mr –"

"Call me Ben. I know he took an interest in your career."

"He didn't have any family, you see. So he was able to help others. There were protégés before me and there were others following." I noted that he fell into the past tense in talking about Horner. Others had too, but Bardell stuck there.

"You were all very fortunate. Have you ever wondered what would have happened to you without Dr Horner's taking an interest in you?"

"Oh, I might be a country doctor someplace. Probably working as hard at that as I am on my pet projects here."

"Can you talk about your research? I never know how secret these things are."

"The general area is urology. I can tell you that. If you're interested, there are a few papers with my name on them in the hospital library. Beyond that, it gets a little technical."

The food had started to arrive, a saucer or two at a time. I recognized some of the dishes as being fancy versions of what I had tasted at Kowloon. I asked the waiter for a knife and fork; that made Bardell smile. In fact, I think that did it. Soon, he was depositing sticky rice on my plate and sharing stories of his life in a village called Burwell, not far from Round Hill. It was a farming community, raising cattle not far from a railway line, which made marketing the milk easier. He told me that he grew up in the house across the road from the mill, and that, as a boy, he'd had fishing rights in the mill race inside the mill.

"Inside?"

"The miller kept a fishing rod in the cellar, close to all the old turbines and penstocks. He made me welcome to it any time the mill was open, which was nearly always. Of course, even in those days, the mill was operated by power from Hydro, so no use was being made of the waterpower. I caught a lot of fish there, mostly trout."

"Well! And you lived across the street. It couldn't've been more convenient."

"There was a character in Burwell, name of Ab Weaver. He always wondered where my trout came from and I never told him. Thought I got them from the mill pond, which was mostly full of catfish and suckers. Ab wasn't quite right in his head. He'd lost two kids, years back, when they shut themselves in a derelict refrigerator and suffocated. When he was drinking, Ab would smash car windows as he staggered home from the pub in town. Provincial police had to lock him up a couple of times. His wife was steady enough. Her people were immigrants, didn't have two red cents to rub together when they settled that part of the township. Ab came from pioneer stock. The original Weaver log house is still being used. Ab used to hate it when I called it a log cabin. 'A log house is what I was born in, which is a step up from the cabin of Abraham Lincoln.' Lot of good it did him."

"Whatever happened to Ab Weaver?"

"I haven't been up that way in ten years. Johnny Plume would know. Johnny ran the general store and played the fiddle in the town band. Laurie Webber, from the Wilder Lake Road, and Johnny were the backbone of that band." Bardell's eyes were gleaming as he told these stories about his younger days and his grammar and pronunciation were making tracks back to those days as well. I refilled his cup with tea from the white pot.

THIRTEEN

An office is much more easily searched than a house, especially for something the size of *A Doctor Remembers*. It took Salter ten minutes the following morning to confirm with Horner's secretary that there was no briefcase or manuscript in his office, and further to confirm that she had no memory of having seen it. Then, as she was closing the communicating door behind her, Salter saw the case, hanging from a coathook on the back of the door. He called the secretary back and pointed at the case. "What on earth…" she began, then lifted the case down. "It's empty."

"Did he usually leave it up there?"

"Never. And it is completely against his character. I mean, hanging your briefcase high on the door is sort of larky, isn't it? He wasn't larky."

They unstrapped the bag and stared at the couple of pencils, a can opener, and a small tin of mints lying loose in the bottom of the bag. Salter waited for the secretary to go away, then picked up the phone to call Vera Denbigh. "Miss Denbigh, would you call together whoever worked on Horner's book and…"

"No one worked on Horner's book. I read it is all. So did Patrick, the editor you met."

"That makes it easier. Would you and Patrick put your heads together and see if you can remember any people in the book who are still around, still active, I mean… ah, no, that could take weeks. I'll have to find another way."

"I think I know what you want, and we already did that. When I realized the people Horner remembered weren't all dead, I showed it to our lawyer with an asterisk against those I thought were still

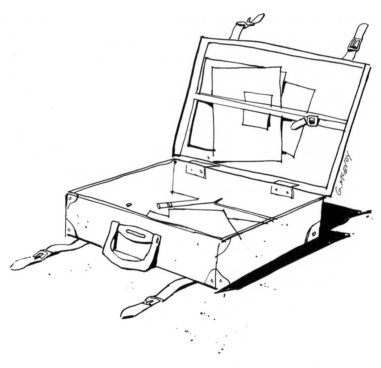

They unstrapped the bag and stared at the couple of pencils...

around. Three of the references he thought were actionable. You want the names?"

"Yes, please."

"Do they then become suspects? Is that how it works?"

"Don't be hasty. I'll suspect them of stealing Horner's manuscript, that's all."

"Why?"

"To protect themselves, I suppose. But they might be useful, or the thief might, because he might be able to tell me where Horner was on the day he disappeared."

"I think you just made that up. Oh, what the hell. Let me close the door again. Here. There's Dr Wimsatt, a surgeon. He's black. Horner called him 'our dusky friend' to conceal his identity. According to Horner he misdiagnosed a case and consequently performed the wrong surgical procedure."

"Cut off the wrong leg?"

"Diagnosed an ectopic pregnancy, operated, and discovered a bleeding ovary instead."

"Let me write that down. E-c-t-o-p-i-c. She die?"

"No, she got an unnecessary scar on her tummy."

"The other two?"

"Dr Leech – yes, truly, her real name – is an obstetrician. Horner has got her involved in an illegal abortion. And the third is another surgeon, a Dr Cooperman, who, according to Horner, engineered a cover-up of a nurse's mistake. But you know, there's nothing sensational about Horner's way of telling the stories; in every case he just lets out pretty alarming stuff – to a layman, anyway – sort of by the way, innocently. He's always primarily telling some other story."

FOURTEEN

Willis Togood was listed in the Yellow Pages as a Private Investigator. The listing came between Investment Services and Invitations and Announcements. My old friend Howard Dover, who used to work the mean streets of Toronto, once recommended Willis to me and when we met I promised to look for work to throw his way. Up until now the promise was more honoured in the breach, as Frank Bushmill is always saying.

I was lucky enough to find Willis at home when I called, and further, he was able to give me the time I needed. I told him about Round Hill and Burwell and Johnny Plume and Ab Weaver. I told him what I knew about Dr Bardell, and what I knew about him, once I saw how fast I was running through it, wasn't much. But Willis is a good fellow and he said he'd see what he could do, which is pretty well what I'd say myself in similar circumstances. He said he'd call me when he had something. I gave him the numbers where he could reach me. Then, after getting a short lecture on the value of cell phones, I was able to get back to work on the breakfast Sue had left me on the kitchen table. The house, halfway up the first block on Brunswick from Bloor, was cool and quiet. It could have been in the middle of the country. I'd missed catching a ride to the hospital with Sam. Resigned, I took my own car and parked it in a lot off McCaul.

I found Sam in his office. "Where the hell have you been all morning?" he demanded. "I didn't invite you here to see the sights. I need your help, Benny. How many times do I have to tell you?"

"Sorry, Sam. I was chatting up Dr Bardell," I lied. "Thought I might learn a thing or two."

"Oh, great! Perfect. Maybe you should go over and stay with him."

"Sam, for crying out loud, what's the matter? I can see you are upset. What's happened?"

"That policeman wants to see me again. You know, Inspector Salter."

"Just sounds like routine. Don't let it worry you."

"You don't know what you're talking about, Benny. Salter knows something."

"What could he know, Sam? What could he possibly know?" Here Sam paused before answering. The longer he paused, the more anxious I became.

"He wants to see me because when I saw him the first time, I was less than frank with him."

"You lied? You fibbed to the Toronto police?" I had forgotten the sheepish look Sam gets when cornered. I remembered the time he filled the punctured tire of my bike with a length of garden hose. Neither Pa nor I was happy with his pretense of innocence.

"Sam, tell me what you said to Salter."

"Right," he said, his lower lip looking slack. "And I have to admit, Benny, I wasn't completely frank with you, either."

FIFTEEN

"Well, well, "Dr Wimsatt said. "First the hospital mislaid old Horner and now you've lost his manuscript. Careless lot, aren't you. How can I help?"

"Have you any idea what was in the manuscript?"

"Not the slightest. The nose-pickings of an old fart of a racist, I assume."

Dr Wimsatt was a big man, medium brown, with a stateless American accent – Californian, perhaps – and a casual manner. Salter found him in an anteroom of the operating theatre, skinning off the green cotton garments of a just-finished operation. "We have an emergency coming up, just for a change," he said. "An old lady fell and broke her elbow about sixteen hours ago. We've been looking for a gap so we can fix her ever since. "

"Sixteen hours!"

"Yes, not bad, is it? Not exactly a walk-in clinic, this. A walking wounded clinic, maybe, but the walking wounded are the medical staff, especially the nurses, trying to cope with a situation they weren't trained for. I mean this is like a fucking field hospital, man, in a bad war. But don't get me started, or we'll spend all day bad-mouthing your government."

"So why don't you go home?" Salter said, trying to be rude.

"Oh, I am home, buddy boy. See, I admire this system, medicare, always have. Home is where the heart is, right? And my heart's right here. Last week a neighbour of mine got an attack of diverticulitis while she was driving through Florida. She spent five hours in the emergency ward while they established it wasn't appendicitis, then they sent her home. They were very thorough. The bill for five hours of checking was five thousand two hundred dollars, American, which the hospital made arrangements to get before they would look at her.

That doesn't happen here yet. It's not the philosophy here, or even the Canadian system I'm complaining about, but the fucking abuse of that system by a bunch of politicians who are bleeding it dry in the most prosperous times this province has seen since the war, all to reduce the taxes of the premier's pals. They've cut us back steadily to the point where – to give a concrete example – the food in this hospital is so bad that the patients' families are regularly bringing in meals the way they did in the last century, all so people like you can get a two-hundred-dollar lollipop, called a tax rebate. What did you do with yours, by the way? Dinner for two at Centro's?"

"I'll ask my wife. Tell me, did your patient die?"

Wimsatt subsided steadily, all passion spent, looked at Salter with his head on one side, and said, "You're a cute one, you know that? No she didn't die, but she will. I couldn't help. Now, what else do you want to know?"

"Dr Horner is missing, and enough time has elapsed that it's starting to look bad. A copy of the manuscript of his book is missing from his office. Several people, including yourself, are badly spoken of in the book."

"What does he say about me?"

"That you once diagnosed a bleeding ovary as an ectopic pregnancy and performed an unnecessary operation."

"That was twenty years ago. Everybody knows the story. I use it as an illustration in my annual lecture to the new interns. Do you think someone like me killed Horner because of what he was writing?"

"It's possible."

The front legs of Wimsatt's chair crashed to the floor. "For Christ's sake, man, I was joking."

"He calls you Dr W in the book."

"Does he?"

"His dusky colleague."

"I told you, he's a racist – harmless, because his particular brand of paternal racism is out of date, but a racist nonetheless. He thinks I have a smaller brain than he has. So you think it was me?"

"Where were you on Saturday?" It was Wimsatt's Americanness , Salter decided, that made him feel as if he was acting in a weekly television serial – "Under the Knife," perhaps.

"Christ, you *are* serious, aren't you?'

"I'm a policeman."

"On Saturday I was in Detroit. I went down on Friday, drove down, got there about two, and came back Sunday. Visiting a friend whose daughter was getting married. I stayed with him. Want his number?"

Salter stood up. "You never saw or heard of Horner's book?"

"No. Is it any good?" Wimsatt smiled.

"It's long, I can tell you that."

* * *

Dr Leech was an obstetrician who at some time had performed an abortion of doubtful legality, which, had all the circumstances been known, might have got her in front of the hospital ethics committee at least. Horner had given this little story the subtitle "The Miracle Worker," and the primary narrative concerned a nurse who seemed to have the power of healing in her hands. Horner told the story as a skeptic obliged to record a chain of events that were inexplicable as science. A young woman, a girl, was having a therapeutic abortion – the pregnancy was a mistake, the result of a casual encounter not typical of the girl, and it was having a violent effect on the girl's mental state. For her own good, Dr Leech and another physician certified the need and scheduled the minor operation. On the way to the operating theatre, the girl experienced an agonizing migraine, and her mother, who was with her, thought the procedure should not go ahead until the girl was comfortable. Then Nurse M arrived, talked to the girl as she lay on the trolley, stroked her forehead with one hand while she cradled her neck with the other, and the pain was lifted. Horner commented, "I had heard of this nurse, and I was deeply skeptical until I was able to observe one of her patients at first hand, both before and after the laying on of the hands, and I became a believer in the power that resides in some people's fingertips."

Thus stated, the account would have been unobjectionable, especially after so much time had passed, but Horner had tried to dramatize and humanize the event by describing the obstetrician and her relationship to the girl, that of a cousin by marriage as well as an inti-mate friend of the girl's mother. To procure an abortion for someone so close brought Leech to the edge of the permissible in those days. Even now it was ethically doubtful. However, when Salter had asked Dr Morgan, the head of medical staff, to arrange an appointment with Dr Leech, he learned that she was retired and for some years had been growing olives in Cadenet in Provence, where she and her hus-band had long owned a small house with an olive grove. This house had become their permanent home.

* * *

That took care of two of the doctors implicated by Horner. The last of the three, Dr Cooperman, had been involved much more recently in covering up a nurse's mistake. Again, the story interested Horner because of the opportunity to philosophize, earnestly but uninter-estingly, on medical ethics. On this occasion two containers of med-ication had changed places on the nurse's medicine trolley, with the result that an elderly patient had received a much stronger sedative than was prescribed, while another geriatric patient lay awake most of the night, waiting for her sleeping pill to kick in. No permanent harm was done, but the nurse, who discovered her own mistake as she sought for the cause of the patients' odd behaviour, immediately called Dr Cooperman. He told the nurse to forget it, but stayed in the area himself to keep an eye on the heavily sedated patient until the next afternoon, when it was certain that the only effect was a slight headache.

SIXTEEN

"Now look, Benny," Sam was saying, "I didn't ask you here just for the fun of it. This is a job, and I expect you to pay attention."

"Sam, I'm not doing my job when I go off half-cocked. I need to be informed in order to perform. You've got to tell me what you said to Salter that's now caught up to you. You've got to tell me what you were less than frank about."

We were sitting on opposite sides of Sam's big desk. He was looking down at me and I was looking up at him. Still, it was Sam who had the anguished look on his face. As far as I could tell, my face was as calm and relaxed as the rest of me. Maybe there was a part of me that failed to appreciate that Sam's life was as real as mine was. His present difficulties had, for me at least, a comic edge to them. He had fibbed and now had been found out. Does an object lesson get any clearer than that?

"Ben, believe me, I would have told you and Salter both, if I hadn't thought it was all water under the bridge, over and done with, dead and buried."

"Yes, so far so good."

"A nurse – never mind her name – came to me after I'd been here for less than two weeks. She was in tears and ready to cut her throat she was so upset. She had reversed two portions of medication. Now this is serious stuff, so I went with her and we monitored the patients concerned through the night and watched for side effects. Both of them made it. It was sloppy medicine; the nurse was shaken by it, but nobody died. Nobody was even in discomfort for very long. It shouldn't have happened, but it did. I talked to the woman for half an hour about the possible repercussions. I could, of course, have brought her name to the attention of my superiors. It would have meant the discipline committee, downgrading, probably dismissal. She was not a careless nurse, Benny, just worked to the hilt while her union was try-ing to make somebody pay attention to the fact that human beings can only be stretched so far. I decided not to make an issue of it. There were no complaints from the two patients or anybody else. So I did nothing, said nothing, and hoped it would go away."

"So, what happened?"

"Nothing happened, until a few days into last week, when Irene Uhyrnuk called to tell me that Horner wanted to see me on Saturday afternoon. I told you the rest. Horner wasn't there."

"What else do you know? There must be something to make you remember this old incident. Maybe it was something else. Maybe you slipped up somewhere else. Or maybe he was going to ask you to take on some new responsibility. Remember, Horner was off-loading some of his responsibilities to younger shoulders. Why are you so sure that this incident of the switched medication had anything to do with it? Maybe it's your guilty conscience."

"On Thursday that nurse involved in the incident spoke to Monica, said that Horner'd paid her a visit. He wanted chapter and verse on the whole schmeer."

"So that's why you think you're sure." I pulled at my ear, hoping that something more reassuring than I could think of then would save the day. The best I could manage was, "Look, Sam, if you tell Salter the story the way you told me, I don't think you have anything to worry about."

"Benny, you don't see! If anything bad has happened to Horner… if he's been kidnapped or murdered, I'm the best suspect Salter has. And the only thing I've got working for me is – well, never mind about that."

"Secrets again! Damn it, Sam, you never learn, do you?"

SEVENTEEN

Dr Horner did not record how he had come to hear of the cases, and Salter guessed from his own experience in the police that at some level they were all common knowledge, folklore, the kinds of stories that are told in cafeterias and nurses' residences. The story of the nurse and Dr Cooperman seemed newer than the others, and Cooperman was still on staff, so Salter asked to see him in Horner's office, which Salter was still using for interviews.

When Dr Cooperman appeared in the doorway of the office, the policeman knew that he had hooked one at last. It was no deep instinct, no trembling of a trained investigator's antennæ that sent Salter the message: to anyone's eyes Cooperman looked ill and worried.

"Come in, doctor, sit down, and tell me when in the last few days you were in this office, and why."

Cooperman showed no surprise at Salter's tactic, and responded in the spirit. "I was looking for the manuscript of Dr Horner's book, the one that gives chapter and verse about a breach of conduct I perpetrated once, something I'm not ashamed of but I don't want on my record."

"Ah, yes, well," Salter said, slightly winded at not getting the two or three sentences of bluster he had been expecting. "Where is the book now?"

"I've destroyed it. In the incinerator."

"Why? It was just a copy. There are others."

"Because you are here about what has happened to Dr Horner, and you will turn over every stone to find it out, and in the course of your search you would come across the manuscript and feel the need to find out if anyone mentioned therein could be sufficiently motivated by what Horner had written to kill him. To do that, you would have to tell the world what I did, and the hospital would have to respond. I don't want that."

"Dr Cooperman, I've read the book, or the bit about you at any rate. Horner wasn't malicious, but he didn't realize the effect of what he was doing, or wanted to do. So what you say is true, but I think we can fix it now. Where were you on Saturday?'

"You questioning me about a murder?"

"I'm trying not to. When did you retrieve the manuscript?"

"Last night. After you left. Late."

"You have a pass key?"

"You left the office open."

"I did what!"

"You left the door unlocked, which I was hoping you'd do. Horner always left it open."

"I left it unlocked?"

"That's how I found it."

Salter said, "Then I guess I must have. That ends my interest in you or the manuscript. Thanks."

When Cooperman was gone, Salter rehearsed the moves he had made before he went home the night before, including locking the door with the key provided by Horner's secretary, which he had put back in her desk drawer, as instructed. That morning, when he arrived, she returned it to him and he had it still, on his own key chain.

EIGHTEEN

Willis Togood had left word with Monica that he wanted to see me later in the day. He had called from Round Hill. "That's near Pickering, isn't it?" asked Monica vaguely, biting into an apple. It was that time in the afternoon when all offices should have inside locks and couches for post-prandial naps. The air stood heavy in the tiny office, and it was crowded; even though we were no longer complete strangers, Monica and I were not on intimate terms.

"Not so far east and further north," I said, not thinking very clearly. I was still digesting what Sam had told me after his meeting with the inspector. There had been a book, and now it had been destroyed. I almost can't imagine Sam doing that, and I almost can. Sam was right, of course: the fact that he had been nailed by Horner in the book and that he had destroyed the book made him a pig's head on a charger with an apple in his mouth. Cops are busy people and justice is an abstraction. I couldn't see how they could avoid picking on my big brother.

But then it came to me that we didn't know who else had it in for Horner. In a big place like this hospital, Sam's couldn't be the only name on the "enemy list." It stood to reason that there must be others. If Salter is a good cop, he'll have a few people besides Sam to bother.

I told Monica that I was going for a walk around the hospital. There were a couple of things I wanted to check. First, I tried all of the doors to see whether they were usually locked or not and made a list as I circumnavigated the old brick structure, with its add-ons on every face, as every new architect had figured a new way to get more beds into the cramped space between the two big hospitals. I counted seven ways out of the building that required a key to come back in the same way and three entrances that were always open in both directions. The front entrance was temporarily closed because of the work being done on the front facade, but it was still possible to get in and out during daylight at least.

On my way back inside, the ivy covering the old walls of the nurses' residence in back looked greener than it had before lunch yesterday. The birds sang sweeter in the trees. It was a fresh, spring-like song, not a tired autumnal one. I may have imagined it, but there was a bounce to my step as I braved the newly arriving traffic at the entrance to Emerg. I went directly to the security office in the main lobby.

"Hello again, Mr Cooperman." Prinsep smiled as he put aside a letter he was reading.

You can tell a lot about someone from the way he greets you across a desk. Some gather their papers before them, letting you know that even saying "hello" is going to put your host behind in his work. "I'll be burning the midnight oil for stealing this time to be cordial to you, you time-waster," they seem to be saying. Others fuss with their papers, letting you know how important they are that they have papers to shuffle and you don't.

"Good to see you. Is there something you'd like to know? You realize that I can't share very much with you, but where I can, I'll always be glad to assist you."

"Do you have a man signing people in and out on weekends, Mr Prinsep?"

"We do. And Dr Horner was signed in on Saturday, but not out."

"How does that mean anything when there are doors that let you out without passing the guard?"

"I didn't invent the system, Mr Cooperman, I inherited it. The architects didn't consult me about creating a secure building. I make do with what I can manage. There are few keys to the small side doors, but, you're right, they offer a free way out. The front door is sealed by the workmen when they finish at five and they didn't work this Saturday."

"That's about what I thought. I wonder if you would help test a theory that has been bugging me for a couple of days."

"If it'll help find Dr Horner, I'm your man."

"I think I know where to find him, Mr Prinsep."

"Well, that is good news."

"Not exactly. If I'm right, Horner's dead."

"Even that's better than not knowing. Does it have anything to do with the doors?"

"No. I was just closing off an alternative possibility. I was in the library over at City Hall on Tuesday, I think, Mr Prinsep, and I saw an old friend of mine: 'The Purloined Letter' by Edgar Allen Poe."

"Old friend of mine, too, Mr Cooperman. What's it got to do with finding the Doc?"

"I say he's in the hospital and not hidden, Mr Prinsep. If he's not on a gurney parked against one of the walls somewhere in a corridor, looking for all the world like a diamond in a crystal jar full of ice, then he has been wheeled into the hospital morgue. You'll find him on a gurney or in one of those refrigerated file drawers."

"How do you know this?"

"Well, when you and your people couldn't find him, then I figured he wasn't in any of the obscure, clever hiding places. That left only the open, public corridors and the morgue. Who would think of looking for a dead man there?"

"I hope you're wrong. I liked Dr Horner. We all did."

"Frankly, I hope I'm wrong too, but I can't see where that might be, Horner being Horner."

"I'll look right into it. Thank you."

"If the post mortem shows that he had some terminal illness, of course, there's a chance that Dr Horner killed himself and put himself on that gurney just to embarrass the government."

"I don't quite follow you."

"Wouldn't it give the hospital and the government a black eye when it became known that a medical man of his repute was allowed to lie dead in a hallway for five days before he was discovered?"

"I'll put my best people on it right away."

NINETEEN

When Horner had not appeared by Wednesday morning, Salter organized two searches, one by his own force to scour the area between the hospital and the College subway entrance, and the streets between Summerhill subway station and Horner's home. The other search was planned to take place within the hospital, and for this one Salter recruited the help of Dr Morgan, who quickly and efficiently broke down the hospital into a dozen areas, finding a supervisor for each, and giving them the job of searching for a lost patient who might be confused and have wandered into a cupboard or unlocked space. The orders were to open every door on to every room in the hospital, the laboratories, the wards, the operating theatres, the storerooms, the closets, and the washrooms. The answer came back immediately: the job had already been done by the security staff; the result was negative.

Now Salter, who had been thinking about hiding places, said, "Have they looked in the morgue?"

Morgan said, "I'll take you there. I know what he looks like."

The hospital morgue was only a holding action, a way station in the disposal of bodies. The bodies were temporarily stored in drawers, just like in the movies, Salter thought.

They found Horner's body in the third drawer the attendant opened, awaiting confirmation of shipping or cremation instructions. The tag on his toe identified him as William Duckworth, and a check through the records showed that William Duckworth had died a week before and his body had been shipped to Aurora, Ontario, for burial. There was no chance that the body in Aurora was not Duckworth. The undertaker knew him personally.

"Is the morgue in your bailiwick?" Salter asked Morgan.

"Why?"

"I was wondering who is in charge of the autopsy, the post-mortem. What's the difference?"

Morgan gestured to dismiss the question without answering it. Salter continued. "I'd like the pathologist – that the word? – to pay special attention to Horner's prostate."

"Why?"

"When we know how he died, we may know that, for instance, he committed suicide. Because he was depressed about his health."

"And lay down in a drawer of the morgue and shut it from the inside, as he died?" Morgan's sneer was spectacular.

Salter smiled back with an equally irritating tolerance. "Don't you read Agatha Christie, sir? That is *exactly* the kind of cute problem she specialized in. But I'll make it easier for you. Our man might have lain down on a trolley in the morgue, put the wrong bracelet on his wrist, one he found in the trash can, say, injected himself with a deadly difficult-to-detect poison (most writers use curare), dropped the needle and stuff into the trash can, which is half full of syringes and other deadly waste material because the hospital is so short of staff the cleaners haven't done the morgue that day yet, and lay down and died. Did he have a remarkable sense of humour?"

"You don't kill yourself for a joke."

"No, and this is the unfunny bit. He killed himself because he had recently been diagnosed with cancer of the prostate, and being a medical man, he knew there was no hope. I have reason to believe, no, I *know* he consulted a urologist in Winnipeg just last week. "

"What for?"

"He was a very private man, I understand."

"Oh, balls. He was a doctor. Hold on. Let me call Blostein." He picked up the phone pressed a button, and dialled a number. "It's Morgan again, David," he said, "And the question is the same. Inspector Salter here wants the pathologist to confirm that Horner had something wrong with his prostate. Will you speak to him? Here he is." He handed the phone to Salter.

"Staff Inspector Salter here."

" I hear the question. Here's the answer. Don't bother the pathologist. Davidson Horner had a perfectly healthy prostate, slightly enlarged but less so than the average for a man his age. Okay? I mean that's what I was saying when I already told Dr Morgan that there was nothing significantly wrong with Horner."

"Then why did he come to you?"

"He didn't. I bumped into him in the hospital when I was checking on a patient and we had a casual conversation in the cafeteria about that damn book he's writing, and went on to the amount of water you should drink in a day, seven glasses the nutritionists say, and he told me he hadn't even had a PSA lately, not in the last couple of years. I'm fond of him. We go back a long way. So he let me check him. There was no evidence of anything wrong. Okay?"

"Thanks." Salter put the phone down.

TWENTY

It took all of the clout he possessed to get the coroner to give Sam a peek at the results of the post-mortem conducted on the body of John Davidson Horner in the bowels of the Forensic Centre on Grosvenor Street some time before midnight on Wednesday. They were doing sensitive tissue analysis on a few organs and other marked areas, but the part I was interested in came out in the first fast look at the last mortal remains of Dr Horner. There was no sign, not even any suspicion, that Horner's prostate was abnormal in any way. Far from being malignant, it was, according to Sam who saw it and spoke of it at dinner on Thursday, rosy and fat, quite the healthiest prostate the pathologist had seen in weeks. A paragon among prostates, in fact. My sister-in-law invited Sam to discuss further examples of unusual anatomical trivia and pathology before the casserole was completely gone. She had hopes of saving some for weekend lunches for the girls.

On Thursday morning I ran into Dr Bardell rushing to the bank of elevators. He told me that the Toronto policeman was not present. He had gone out of town. I was highly curious where he had gone, but I decided I could live with it for a few minutes. Big institutions are like islands: you can't keep a secret for long. If you see a secret being whispered to a second person across a room, there's no need to lean closer to overhear. You're bound to hear what it was all about before sundown. Now, my knowledge of islands is scanty, but I read about them, and next to travel, reading is the next most broadening pastime.

Now there was yellow "Crime Scene" tape over the entrance to Horner's office. Irene had bunked in with Monica Levine, which couldn't have brightened the day for either one of them. "Welcome to Club Millionaire!" Monica sang out in a cheery voice. "I hope you brought your own olive oil."

"I hope you're both dolphin safe," I said. "Anything new here at the hospital?"

"This formal notice came around announcing Dr Horner's death this morning," Irene said, handing over a black-edged sheet of paper.

"Signed by Fred O'Donahue," I noted.

"Reversed borders for mourning. Black letter type. All the right touches," added Irene, who, despite her irony, looked like she was taking it hard.

"Has anyone been talking to his sister?"

"O'Donahue called her and he asked me to call her as well. I did that twenty minutes ago. She's going to be fine. Glad the waiting and uncertainty is over."

"Where's Toronto's finest?" I knew the answer, but you never know what interesting answers you can pick up by asking dumb questions.

"Oh, didn't you hear? He took off for Winnipeg as soon as the post-mortem results were in."

"Winnipeg?"

"That's what I said." Irene nodded to affirm the truth of that.

Monica went on: "When the inspector gets back, he wants to see Sam again. Sam knows about it. I think you should talk about it together. He's worried."

"Has he come in yet?"

"Come and gone. Our day starts early, Mr C. Sam's over at TGH for a consultation. He should be back after lunch."

"I think I'll scout around for coffee."

"If I take my empty cup out of Monica's office, you might be able to squeeze a full cup in."

"Probably not with my two spoonfuls of sugar. I'm going to try to find Dr Bardell. Wonder how he's taking the news. I just saw him running for a meeting and didn't have time to quiz him."

"If you're lucky," Irene Uhrynuk said, checking her watch, "you'll find him coming out of the Research Grants meeting in the third-floor boardroom at a quarter to twelve. You only have forty minutes to kill."

"Be careful, he usually tries to find somebody who'll invite him to lunch."

"He's not going to catch me again. That first one cost me an arm and a leg."

Irene was making a strange face. Monica caught it first; I was a little slow. "There's a little man who keeps walking by the doorway," she whispered.

"Well, we're full up in here," announced Irene. Monica tilted her chair to the upright position and began trying to get past us. "I'll sort him out," she said. In thirty seconds, she flicked her head into the doorway. "He wants you, Benny. Says you know him." I got to my feet as quickly as I could, and with a little moving on Irene's part, I was free of the sardine can.

It was Willis Togood. He was leaning against the opposite wall, between two gurneys with ivs running. "Benny," he said in a voice that was both hoarse and nervous. "I got the gen you wanted." Willis was wearing a brown corduroy suit. It was rumpled. When I referred to it as brown, he corrected me. "Anthracite," he said.

"Good. Let's get some coffee."

When we were both furnished with a warm mug between our hands, I nodded that it was now the time. "How do you want this?" he asked. "Long or short?"

"Give me your sources first, then I'll take the rest neat."

"Daniel Hughes, school principal, Burwell; John Plume, retired storekeeper, Burwell; adoption records, Round Hill. That's about it."

"And?"

"There are holes in it, Ben. It's not airtight. But this is the way it looks. Clive Russell Bardell was born in Round Hill. You need the year?" I shook my head. "He was adopted by Sydney and Alexandra Bardell, English immigrants from Burpham, Sussex, near where my nephew Simon lives, and brought up in and around Burwell, Ontario, until he was sent to Upper Canada College. Who paid the shot? Same person who helped him with his tuition at University of Toronto, same person who gave him up for adoption in the first place: John Davidson Horner. Looks like Doc Horner had sprouted a wild oat."

TWENTY ONE

Morgan was waiting for Salter to go so he could get on with his work. Salter said, "That answers that, then. But maybe you could do me a favour. Would you get me a copy of the report on the post-mortem, and, in the light of our little chat about Agatha Christie, read it yourself first – suspiciously, I mean – and tell me anything that seems unusual."

Morgan dropped his attitude and looked intrigued. "All right. Yes, I'll be glad to. And I'll have a chat with the pathologist. This is interesting. Where can I find you?"

Where would he be?

"I'm going to Winnipeg right now, as soon as I can get a plane. I'll be back tomorrow." Salter had just realised that with the time difference between Winnipeg and Toronto, and if he was lucky with a plane connection he could be in Winnipeg in time for lunch and have the afternoon to track down Horner's shipboard companion to find out why Horner, a man with no apparent medical problems, flew to Winnipeg suddenly to consult a urologist.

* * *

Salter took a cab from the airport to the Fort Garry General Hospital, where he found Dr Grierson, Horner's cruise companion, waiting for him in his office.

"It's my lunchtime," Grierson said," and the only time I have to talk to you until late this afternoon. Have you eaten? No? Then let's pick up a sandwich in the cafeteria and lock the door."

Ten minutes later Salter unwrapped his sandwich, took a bite, and said, "I think I said it all on the phone. Your friend Dr Horner is dead. He was found in a drawer in the morgue, almost certainly killed, by persons unknown, for reasons similarly unknown. I found out he had been consulting you..."

Grierson said nothing.

Salter continued. "Everyone told me what a private man he was, so I assumed that the reason must be a medical one he didn't want to share with his colleagues. What other reason could he have for flying out to talk to a man he had met on board a ship two years ago?"

"Horner's visit to me had nothing to do with his health. It had to do with a research project at his hospital. I had been informed that there were things about it that Horner was not aware of. I might not have bothered, but I grew fond of Davidson that week we spent together – he's a type that is dying out – and he didn't need another scandal after the last episode. So I called him."

"First of all, how did you hear about it, whatever it is?"

"We had a new man join the research staff. He told me. He didn't want to – people are very close-mouthed, protective, in this profession. Point is, the guy we hired left Rose of Sharon because he didn't like the way this particular piece of research was being conducted, and he had to tell me because I wanted to know why he was moving from the centre of the universe to Winnipeg." Grierson did not smile, leaving Salter to figure out the degree of irony he was employing. "Now, Inspector, I fulfilled my ethical duty by letting Davidson know something was rotten in his state. That was all I think I needed to do. After that, I assume that he took over. Frankly, I want to keep my involvement down to just that, unless I am subpoenæd or something."

"It might save you having to fly to Toronto one day, if you would give me some idea of what it's all about."

Grierson made the desk-squaring motions of a man who has spent enough time on a problem, and now wants to move on. "I'll try for an analogy. It's as if just before you go into court to testify, you realize that a little piece of evidence is missing, hasn't been confirmed, and when you inquire it turns out that someone has been tampering with the evidence, just a little bit, to save time, but just enough to make the whole case suspect. There was also a question of accounting, how the money was spent, but I know nothing about that. That's it. More you'll have to get from someone else."

TWENTY TWO

After he had reported his findings, I wrote out a cheque for Willis, who left a copy of the file with me. Later, I was sorry I didn't walk him down to the nearest exit and not leave him to run the gamut through Emerg. But I was incapable of moving just then. The chair had clutched my innards, as only a hospital chair can, and I just sat and waited for five, or maybe it was ten, minutes staring at the fast-food choices standing above the cafeteria's long open window hatch. I could hear the usual snippets of conversation echoing around my head:

"I went in with the intention of being radical. I had to be..."

"... told her about the non-surgical alternatives..."

"... got it all, I told them..."

"Mr Cooperman?"

"What?" For a moment it was Sam, replaying our meeting last Tuesday. But the voice wasn't Sam's. I tried to focus my eyes. Red geese on a blue background. The necktie was settling down opposite me, where Willis Togood had been sitting. The shirt looked like it had been slept in. The jacket was blue tweed and in need of a press. I caught recently clipped eyebrows, a ruddy complexion, and a smile that seemed to know more than it said.

"You know who I am?" he asked. I didn't get my answer assembled in time to beat him to the utterance. "Charlie Salter," he said. "Don't I know you?"

"Maybe, but it's from years back. You must have been passing through. I haven't worked in Toronto until a couple of years ago." He was carrying a mug of coffee with him as he settled, watching me. Lank grey hair hung over his forehead. Crows feet extended his eyes back towards the tops of his ears. It was a good face for a policeman.

"I just got back from Winnipeg," he said settling his weight into the chair. I nodded. I didn't think he would answer the question forming in my head, so I didn't ask what he found out there.

"What was his name? Grierson? I can't remember."

"Doesn't matter, I reckon. I think I've got all the pieces now."

"You will when we've finished talking," I said. I took a sip from my mug, noticing for the first time how strong the brew was. Now he was doing the nodding.

"Travelling Business Class swells my legs," he said. "I can feel it under my knees. Hurts like billy-oh."

"Where shall we start? You weren't fooled by Sam's little game?"

"Oh, no. I knew you had him mostly battened down. For about ten seconds, he looked like he was a keeper, but he hadn't locked Horner's door after he took the manuscript. That was a bit silly, but I'm not sure what I'd do if some crackpot amateur writer started writing my unauthorized biography. Are you?"

"Save me from writers," I said.

"A good paraphrase of what that publisher woman said. I think you're both right."

"Fill me in on her later. I could scare her with talk of a seven hundred dred page manuscript of my own."

"You'd give her conniptions."

We talked it all out at the table in the hospital cafeteria. Men and women in operating room greens came in with their face masks dangling. They ate sandwiches and drank coffee. They came, left, and were replaced by others. First I listened to Charlie and then Charlie listened to me. He was easy to think of as Charlie. And I didn't notice when he started calling me Benny. Neither of us interrupted much, but you could feel the story growing in solidity as we filled in the pieces at the end.

"Will you come up with me to talk to the sister? Her name is Plum."

"Isn't this your show from here on?" I asked him.

"Not necessarily. We can do a dog and pony act. She'll give us biscuits."

"What about Bardell?"

"Oh, he's already taken care of as far as his fiduciary irregularities go. The rest can come later."

"Well, if you think I won't put the old girl off, I'd be glad to come."

"I've got a car downstairs."

He didn't have to take me, of course, and most of the cops I know would have sent me on my way. But Charlie was his own man, and besides, he was acknowledging that I had done half the work. I just wanted to watch the last act, to see if there were any more surprises.

We talked it all out at the table in the hospital cafeteria.

TWENTY THREE

They went to the Horner residence in Salter's car. He couldn't see any reason to tell Cooperman to go away, back to Grantham, or wherever he came from. Cooperman had saved Salter a lot of work, although Salter knew they would have got to the same place in the end. Grierson, the urologist in Winnipeg, knew about Bardell, though he hadn't named him, and Salter would have got Dr Hui to eliminate every other researcher eventually.

Horner's sister opened the door, nodded to Salter, and looked quizzically at Cooperman. "This is your trusty but not very bright sergeant?" she asked. "As in all the best TVO serials?"

Salter said, "No, ma'am. He's too short and too bright," and then introduced Cooperman to her.

"The name is familiar," she said. "Come inside."

"I wish it were a household word," Cooperman said. "But I just work out of Grantham. Hard to get your name on everybody's lips when you're from the wine region, unless your name's Inniskillen."

She smiled politely to acknowledge Cooperman's self-mockery. "Not you. Your name. Someone with your name. A colleague of Davidson's, whom he greatly respected. He put an anecdote about him in his book. Any relation?"

"My brother. And that's an anecdote that might get him doctoring up in North Bay for the rest of his life. That was your brother's idea of admiration?"

She looked glum for a moment. "I've talked to Vera Denbigh about the book. It certainly won't be published now, of course. But the stories were not badly intended. Quite the reverse. It's just that Davidson was in some ways a fool. Now what are we here for? You've found out something you think I should have told you, and you've come to ask why I didn't tell you, right? Why? Why should I have told you? Tell me."

Salter said, "We've found your brother's body."

"In the hospital, where I told you to look in the first place. How? Where?"

"In the morgue."

"I told you from the start that he had probably suffered a heart attack and was lying somewhere out of sight."

"Someone killed him. He was murdered."

Salter saw all the control she had inherited from her race and class and upbringing being brought to bear on news that should have rendered her hysterical, howling with grief, at least stunned. She paled slightly. "I see," she said. "Do you know who it was? Who did it?"

"I think you might tell me, ma'am, and I think you might have suggested it a few days ago."

Now she exploded, but only like an outraged citizen. "Why? Why should I have told you? It only matters to me, and my private life is my concern. If I'd told you, it would have been in the newspapers by now and so would I. I don't know if I could have adapted to that. The hell with you."

"If you had told me about Clive Bardell, it would have helped me to avoid suspecting everyone else."

"I might not have cared that much. It would have done that oily tinker Fred O'Donahue good to have spent a few weeks as one of those suspected of murder. I should have enjoyed that."

"What about Dr Cooperman?" Salter asked.

"Sam? Oh, no. Oh, no. No, of course you're right. I ought to have told you everything, I suppose. Is there anything left you don't know? Perhaps I can make amends."

Cooperman started to speak, but Salter put a hand out to keep him quiet. "Just confirm the facts. Did you know that your brother was about to end Bardell's career?"

"Not before time. Bardell betrayed my brother's trust in him."

"In spite of their relationship?"

She sat still, her eyes darting from Salter to Cooperman, waiting for the word, saying nothing.

"In spite of the fact that Bardell knew himself to be your brother's son?"

She said, "And used the knowledge to try and blackmail Davidson? He didn't know my brother very well. But I hear what you are saying. Bardell killed my brother because Davidson wouldn't do what he wanted and therefore Bardell was finished."

"Even though he was your brother's son."

"Presumably. You're sure of that, are you?"

"I guess blood tests, DNA tests, stuff like that will nail it down. And we'll probably look for the mother."

"You won't have to look far."

A splutter from Benny made Salter realize he had got there at the same time as his cohort.

"Jesus," Benny said. "Are you saying that…" His mouth was wide open.

"Let Miss Horner explain, Benny."

"The hell with that," she said. "The hell with that. Tell the story yourself."

"What a story," Cooperman said.

Now she conceded. "All right. Bardell is my son, God rot him. And now I suppose the world will know and I'll have to endure a retirement full of whispers and sidelong looks. I don't care, but my fiancé will. He's led a sheltered life in that library."

"Maybe you should tell him yourself," Cooperman suggested.

"Maybe I should *what*? You think he doesn't know? I wouldn't dream of deceiving him. I told him the whole story when he proposed, six years ago. I wanted to know then if it made any difference, but of course it didn't." She smiled a bit. "James just said it was the sort of thing the slightly headstrong streak he had detected in me would cause, and one of the reasons he wanted to marry me. Oh, no. It's just other people knowing that James wouldn't like, as I wouldn't. But there's no help for it now, is there? The whole gripping story will wind up on *Newsworld*. They will even try to track down Clive's actual biological father, I suppose, but they'll have trouble. Now that Davidson is dead, only I know that, and James doesn't want to."

She watched Salter's face and shook her head slowly and carefully.

"You can put that out of your head. There's nothing as lurid as that. Poor Davidson. They've been speculating about his sexual orientation all his life, and now they'll throw me into the mix, even if just to deny it, the way some of them can. Oh, God, what a jolly time I've got to look forward to."

Salter looked at Cooperman. "You want to wait in the car?"

"If you have some way out of this for all of us, I want to hear it," he replied. "If I step out of line, you can step on *me*. I know that. I'm with you and I think I know what's coming."

So Cooperman was safe enough.

"Miss Horner, maybe the story needn't all be told. Tell us about the professional relationship between Bardell and your brother," Salter continued.

"I'm not sure I can be sufficiently objective. The truth is, I didn't like my son. I didn't know him until recently and what I knew I didn't like. Let me tell you my story. When I was in first year Oberlin, I lost my head and became pregnant by a boy from Columbus, Ohio..."

"Where was that? Overland?" Cooperman cut in.

"Oberlin. It's a liberal arts college in Ohio. Davidson paid for me to go there. Well, I got pregnant and I called Davidson to tell him I was going to kill myself and he came down and solved everything, found a way for me to get through the time, found a family to adopt the baby, and got me enrolled the following year in Victoria College here, and no one was any the wiser. It took a lot of managing, and it brought me and Davidson very close. He continued to regard himself as responsible for Clive, and you know the rest."

"No question of an abortion?" Cooperman asked. "Your brother against it?"

She nodded. "I would have had one like a shot, but Davidson wouldn't hear of it. In some ways he's more Catholic than that hospital he works in. So I had the baby, gave it up, and never saw him again until Davidson hired him at the hospital. Davidson had been monitoring his progress all along, as I say, and supplying the funds, anonymously."

"Why?" Salter asked.

"His sense of responsibility. I was responsible, and therefore he, my brother, was responsible."

"Bardell had no idea of the truth, did he?"

"Not until the law changed and he was allowed to find out who his natural parents were. At that point, his relationship with Davidson changed. My brother continued to support him through medical school, but now he thought he knew who his father was, Bardell became rather relaxed with him and less grateful."

"Did you get to know him then? What was you impression of him?"

"I knew who he was, of course, but I never saw him except at a distance, never wanted to. He was an accident that my brother did his best to compensate for. I had no maternal feeling, and no curiosity. If I had any feelings about it, I was angry at having to exchange Oberlin, which I loved, for Victoria College. Otherwise, as far as his reappearance was concerned, I didn't want to know. Except for not being able to marry James yet, I liked my life and didn't want it disturbed."

"So what can you tell me about their professional relationship?"

"Nothing. We didn't speak of Clive at home. I knew something was troubling Davidson lately, but I didn't know it involved Clive. What had he been up to?"

"That's what I have to find out."

"Do you really think you can keep my story out of the papers?"

"It'll depend on Bardell. I'll try."

"Will you at least let me know if you fail before the world knows."

"I'll call you."

"Can I come?" Cooperman asked. "I think I'm entitled to hear this part too!"

"Oh, yes. I need you to watch while I ask the questions. Just don't interrupt."

Salter called Bardell and arranged to meet him in Horner's office.

She sat still, her eyes darting from Salter to Cooperman, waiting
for the word, saying nothing.

Salter took a final swig of coffee and set his mug down on the kitchen table.

"We fenced for about an hour before Bardell broke down. Then we made a deal."

Salter was at home, telling Annie the story.

"But Annie, you should have seen him try to brace himself and organize his resistance, until he suddenly reached the point where he could see it was a waste of time. Then I went as far as I could in letting him know that I had developed a personal interest in the matter, a desire to keep his mother's connection to the case out of it, and I pointed out all the advantages of keeping the matter simple, just something that happened between him and Horner. Benny helped, elaborating on how messy things could get otherwise, and how irritated this would make the cops, while I stepped out of the room, supposedly to sharpen a pencil."

"Does anyone actually sharpen pencils anymore?" Annie responded.

"When I came back into the room, Bardell and I got his story clear, and I brought him in to be booked."

"And this private eye? Did he go back to Grantham?" Annie asked, as she started flipping through a travel brochure.

"I wanted to buy Benny dinner to celebrate, but he couldn't leave Toronto fast enough. He said he had an urgent case of insurance fraud to investigate. Something about a guy in a wheelchair as a result of an accident at work, last seen playing hockey."

From: Staff Inspector Salter
To: Deputy Chief Mackenzie
Re: Dr D Horner

I'm working on the official report, but here is the summary you requested. I've kept it very informal on the assumption that it's for your eyes only.

Dr Horner was first reported missing on Monday, September 10. His body was found on Wednesday, September 12, in the morgue. A puncture wound was found in his neck. The post-mortem revealed the presence of poison. (See attached report by the investigating pathologist. Some of these reports, like this one, are in their final form.)

The suspect, Dr Clive Bardell, is now in custody. What follows is substantially what took place at the interview with Bardell (see transcript of interview attached).

I was accompanied in the final stages of the inquiry, during the interviews with Miss Horner (see attached) and with Bardell, by a private investigator from Grantham, Mr Benjamin Cooperman. I let him be present because he had brought valuable evidence to me as the result of a parallel investigation he was conducting on behalf of his brother, Dr Samuel Cooperman (see attached). His doctor brother was concerned that he had once upon a time infringed in a minor way on the code of professional ethics he is supposed to uphold, and he had asked his brother to help him assess the danger to him if the story of his little infraction should get out. I have set all this out in a separate document (see attached) but what matters is that in trying to become familiar with his brother's situation, real and imagined, this private eye uncovered the fact that Dr Bardell and Dr Horner (the victim) were related by blood. Cooperman assumed that Bardell was Horner's illegitimate son, as I did, which would account for the favours Horner had shown him. But we later learned that Horner was sterile, had been since a child, and so in putting these two facts together, it became evident that Bardell was Miss Horner's son, not the doctor's, a secret that had been kept for more than thirty years.

Miss Horner confirmed this (see attached).

Based on these facts, I interviewed Bardell and he confessed to the murder.

The essence of his story is as follows. (I knew much of it already – see attached interview with Dr Grierson of the Fort Garry General Hospital in Winnipeg. Bardell only confirmed it.)

Bardell had been brought on staff as a research director to conduct a project, testing a new drug to be used for treating diseases of the prostate. Apparently his methodology was questionable, and so he was questioned by Dr Horner, who had been alerted by a colleague in Winnipeg. There was also a failure to account for all the funds that had been allocated to the project.

Dr Horner confronted his protégé, Bardell, and ordered him to close the project down and resign. Horner offered to help him find work elsewhere in some other field.

At this point, Bardell threatened Horner that if Horner exposed him he would tell the world about their (Horner's and Bardell's) relationship. He did not know that Horner was not, in fact, his father: all along, Horner had been protecting his sister, knowing that at least one other doctor knew that Horner was sterile, and the publicity, the thing that Horner and his sister most shrank from, would be very fierce.

Nevertheless, Horner grew so angry at being blackmailed that he withdrew even his small offer of help, never mind what Bardell might say about their relationship, and told Bardell to resign immediately because he intended to inform the Board of Governors that they had to cancel his research project, and why.

Bardell now knew that he had underestimated Horner's integrity, that the game was up, and he left Horner's office, returning an hour later with the murder weapon, the hypodermic needle. Then, using a hospital gurney and dressing (both himself and Horner's body) in hospital coveralls to render them anonymous, he transferred the body to the morgue. (The arrangements he made were complicated; Bardell was both clever and lucky. See attached.)

There should be no difficulty proceeding with this case. Bardell admits his guilt; he has signed a statement (see attached), and we have the hypodermic complete with his fingerprints.

Now, sir, in what follows I am exceeding my responsibility to make a recommendation for you to pass on to the lawyers. It is, briefly, that Bardell be charged simply with killing Horner in a fit of rage because Horner, in uncovering Bardell's behaviour, had ruined his career. The alternative, involving the revelation in court of the relationship of Bardell to Miss Horner, and the attempt at blackmail, and all the crap that prosecutors get up to to smear witnesses, would only hurt innocent parties – including Miss Horner, her fiancé, Dr Cooperman, and various others. Bardell agrees it would do him no good. Also, Horner was working on a book, A Doctor Remembers, which, if the details ever became public, would cause an awful lot of misery. All this can be kept under wraps, and should be, being in everyone's interest including, I suppose, Bardell's. (At least we can get the fact that he cooperated with the police into the record. One day, when he comes up for parole, it might help.)

Let the lawyers confer.

Mr Fred O'Donahue, Chairman of the Board
Rose of Sharon Hospital
559 University Avenue
Toronto, Ontario, M5G 1X9

Dear Mr O'Donahue,
The Research Committee has now met with the Munn Foundation and it has been decided that it would be in the best interest of the hospital and our other research projects that remain ongoing to abandon the Dymar-Cal project where it stands. I have stopped all funding as of the 30th Inst., and it only awaits a final accounting to terminate this section and leave the space free for other necessary work. Should I not hear from you by tomorrow or Friday, I will proceed as discussed and will send you the final report when it becomes available.

With all good wishes,
Paul Hui, Chief Research Officer

Darling Plum,

We've waited long enough. Bardell kept his word at the trial and now you must keep yours. Last week I got mother into Preakness House, and now that your brother is gone, there is nothing in our way. (I've spoken to Hart House, the chapel is ours for the asking.) Six friends each, we agreed, and a wedding breakfast at Le Select, if they'll have us. Sell both houses, start fresh somewhere new. What about a week Saturday?

Yours, my dear,
James

Dear Sam,

I'm sorry I made a hasty retreat from the fleshpots of Silver City, Sam. Please thank Sue for me and I was sorry I didn't get a chance to at least take the girls to a movie. But I've been invited back for Thanksgiving, so I'll see you all again then.

By the way, I've been assured by Inspector Salter that there will be no follow-up on anything that you were concerned with in this case. In order to keep the case as simple as possible, the sidebar items, like your brave defence of that forgetful nurse, and the mysterious disappearance of Dr Horner's memoir, will not be brought into the record. Once again, fame slips through your fingers.

Don't forget to send a card for Ma's seventy-fifth. See you in a couple of weeks,

Benny

HOWARD ENGEL was born in Toronto and raised in St. Catharines, Ontario. He later lived in Nicosia, London, and Paris, where he worked as a journalist and broadcaster. Back in Canada he was for many years a distinguished producer for the CBC.

His engaging private eye, Benny Cooperman, has been described as a cherished national institution, and many of his novels have been translated into other languages.

Howard Engel is a member of the Mystery Writers of America and the British Crime Writers' Association, and is a founding member of the Crime Writers' Association of Canada. He was the 1990 winner of the Harbourfront Festival Prize for Canadian literature and the 1984 winner of the Arthur Ellis Award for crime fiction. Mr Engel was a Barker-Fairley Distinguished Visitor in Canadian Culture at the University of Toronto.

ERIC WRIGHT was born in London, England, and emigrated to Canada. After earning degrees at the Universities of Manitoba and Toronto, working in construction and as a guide at a fishing camp to pay his way, he became an instructor at Ryerson Institute of Technology in Toronto. There he served as a professor, chair of the English department, and Dean of Arts. He began to write, first for periodicals and television, and his first Charlie Salter mystery won the John Creasey Award from the Crime Writers Association of England. Two subsequent mysteries in that series won the Arthur Ellis Award for Best Mystery published in Canada, as did two of his short stories, and he also won the City of Toronto Book Award.

Canada's most honoured mystery writer, Eric Wright retired from teaching ten years ago, but is "still writing novels." He lives with his wife and near his two daughters in Toronto.

GREG McEVOY is a Toronto commercial artist, illustrator,
He also works in print advertising and film producti
storyboards, layouts, logo designs, computer graphics,
caricatures. He is the author/illustrator of *Alfie's Long Win
Cream King* for Stoddart Kids and a contributing illustrato
Youth Employment Services Guide (Stoddart) and Lee M
Science series (Somerville House).

Mr McEvoy was raised on a dairy farm in the Ottav
now lives and works in downtown Toronto.

GREG McEVOY is a Toronto commercial artist, illustrator, and designer. He also works in print advertising and film production, creating storyboards, layouts, logo designs, computer graphics, cartoons, and caricatures. He is the author/illustrator of *Alfie's Long Winter* and *The Ice Cream King* for Stoddart Kids and a contributing illustrator to *Good Job! Youth Employment Services Guide* (Stoddart) and Lee Marek's *Weird Science* series (Somerville House).

Mr McEvoy was raised on a dairy farm in the Ottawa Valley. He now lives and works in downtown Toronto.